Bitter Rose

Bitter Rose

A novel by

MARTINE DELVAUX

TRANSLATED BY DAVID HOMEL

Cover design: Debbie Geltner
Cover image: Eléonore Delvaux-Beaudoin
Author photo: Patrick H. Harrop
Book design: WildElement.ca

Printed and bound in Canada.

Library and Archives Canada Cataloguing in Publication

Delvaux, Martine, 1968-
[Rose amer. English]
        Bitter rose : a novel / by Martine Delvaux ; translated by David Homel.

Translation of: Rose amer.
Issued in print and electronic formats.

ISBN 978-1-927535-56-1 (pbk.).--ISBN 978-1-927535-59-2 (pdf).—
ISBN 978-1-927535-57-8 (epub).--ISBN 978-1-927535-58-5 (mobi)

I. Homel, David, translator II. Title. III. Title: Rose amer. English.
PS8607.E495R6713 2015   C843'.6   C2014-906290-7
                                                C2014-906291-5

The publisher gratefully acknowledges the support of the Canada Council
for the Arts and of SODEC.

Linda Leith Publishing Inc.
P.O. Box 322, Station Victoria, Westmount QC H3Z 2V8 Canada
www.lindaleith.com

To my mother
To my missing father
To the missing children

I came into a world where no one spoke of men, they were not a subject of conversation because they didn't really exist, or only as grandfathers, bosses, neighbours, doctors. Life was lived among girls. There was my grandmother and her slow-witted but malevolent sisters. There was my mother who worked all the time. And there was me. With us, sometimes, was the downstairs neighbour who had long blond hair that fell like a waterfall onto her shoulders, and she would tie it at the back of her neck. That made her head look completely round, but with a fishtail in back. She wore bell-bottom pants and tight sweaters with no bra underneath. Sometimes she'd take me in for a while to give my mother a break. Her name was Diane like Diane Dufresne, the singer. She described every detail of the extravagant dresses she wore on stage and taught me to sing *Aujourd'hui j'ai rencontré l'homme de ma vie*. She was full of love, she was kind, she didn't have children, and she talked to little girls the way grown-ups talk to other grown-ups. It was always quiet in her house, she would say, "You're a breath of fresh air" and compare me to a young Beaujolais. Those days were filled with tiny toys fished out of the bottom of cereal boxes in the morning, Cracker Jack that broke your teeth, sticky Rice Krispies squares, chicken sandwiches that were impossible to dip into the gluey Saint Hubert sauce, melting choco-late sundaes topped with peanuts from Dairy Queen. Life was like a fairy tale. The princes were away, and one day they would suddenly appear after having fought a drag-on. Saturday Prince Charming, Sunday the Prodigal Son, the rest of the week you wait.

On the evening of July 1st, my mother would wake me up to watch the colourful explosions of the fireworks, I was half asleep at my bedroom window so high in the sky that it floated. That was before the village. That was before my second life. I was still wearing my blue flan-nelette pajamas, I carried my pink blanket with the satin ribbons everywhere I went, it was cool to the touch, its silky weave was full of bumps, a kind of popcorn stitch you make if you knit very very tight. In that world, men were pale stars in distant orbit and far from us, destined to fade out in the blind stain of the universe. People said that life was a thing you had to face on your own, you couldn't expect anything from men, or not very much. There was the story of the one who had left. That was no secret for us, it was a secret for other people, a story full of holes. People said he was tall, he had green eyes like a lake whose bottom is invisible, algae between your toes and soft, gluey mud you sink into far enough to be afraid you'd get stuck. People said it wasn't the first time, he'd done that kind of thing before, he'd known his share of girls. People said he wore wooden shoes and came from houses that waltzed upon the water. People said he had yellow hair and that he must have gone back to his country, where everyone had yellow hair the way he did.

The evening she came to show him her belly like a crystal ball, my mother laid siege to his bachelor apartment among the dirty sheets, cigarette butts, empty beer bottles, and a vague smell of grass and patchouli. She finally fell asleep, and when she awoke the next morning, she realized he was gone. She spent the day turning circles in the little apartment. She was waiting for him, or pretending to. She opened the drawers, rummaged through the closets, understood that his passport had disappeared, and an old suitcase with his money. He was a little crook, my grandfather had seen it right off, but his words were lost. My father blew away in the wind like the dandelion fluff that covers the lawn with a white blanket in spring.

He was a Coca-Cola drinker and a James Bond fan, he'd set a meeting then stand you up. At best, he showed up hours late, disappeared again without saying he was leaving, and you could never tell when he would be back. His friends had long hair and wore paisley shirts. Strangers left messages for him at Johnny's, the corner store, hidden words he would pick up between two pages of the *Journal de Montréal* when he went to buy a pack of menthol cigarettes that my mother ended up smoking. We finally figured out he was a driver for illegal businesses, the soft drug trade, or stolen goods that moved back and forth across the border.

It was 1968, five hundred thousand American soldiers were bogged down in Vietnam, NYU was on strike, Martin Luther King got assassinated. There was nothing that unusual about being an unwed mother, but for my grandmother, who had dreams of a higher social standing, it was a national catastrophe, as disastrous as the future election of the Parti Québécois. Everyone knew the facts: all or nearly all fathers were absent, travelling salesmen, lost in the fields or the streets of some big city, carried off in the fog of alcohol or the arms of a mistress who smoked little cigars and drank whisky after making love in black lace garters. But my grandmother was furious, she raised her arms heavenward and asked what she had done to deserve such a calamity, it was like a rain of vermin or a cloud of locusts, God's wrath in the Old Testament. Family honour must be saved, a story had to be invented to conceal the banality of seeds carelessly sown.

My grandmother wasn't the kind of woman to mince words, and thirty years later, in her mouth, the taste is still fresh. Coldly, without shame or regret, she described how she banished her daughter from the house to keep from lapsing into depression. She sent her to live out her pregnancy elsewhere, far from Montreal and the neighbours' eyes, like Cosette abandoned by the roadside, anything to

4

hide the truth. My young mother dragged herself and her belly to Quebec City. One night, her friends wouldn't let her go to the movies with them. They were going to see *Rosemary's Baby*, why add the devil to the fact that she was going to have a little bastard? When it came time for me to come into the world, gazing upon her body racked with pain, the nurse told her, "That's nothing, my girl. Wait! The worst is yet to come!" My mother was asleep by the time I stuck my nose out. When we met, I'd already been born, I had a head start on her.

A few streets from there, the orphanage opened its doors wide to ruined girls. That was a first migration, a week there like in a hotel, an intermediate stop between the hospital and the ordinary world until my mother could take back control of her destiny. Offering the little package to the sisters, she must have trembled as she implored them not to make a mistake, they shouldn't give the baby away, just look after it until the father came back or the grandmother choked down her bile. In the end, the family's Cadillac appeared like in a version of *Love Story* where love doesn't win out but a forced sense of duty does, complete with tightly clenched teeth. The car was as black as a hearse. It made the return trip from Quebec City to Montreal, and everyone went back to square one. Some things never change.

My grandmother refused to open the living room curtains for fear of what people might say. She said no to everything and insisted on having a dutiful child under her roof. My grandmother was proud, and out of pride, she was perfectly capable of nastiness. Upright, rigid, cutting, a piece of flint, a stone, she swore by her diamond rings, her designer suits, her golden necklaces, the Lord in heaven, and a litany of principles whose mission was to preserve the straight and narrow in this vile world perverted by time. My grandmother was one of those women who love their daughters when they are far away. They don't love them when they are sick or in pain, pregnant or needy. They love them in their absence. Only then could love give them wings. When my mother returned, life went on like before.

My grandmother harboured a world of secrets she needed to conceal in order to keep up appearances, whatever the price. She was a woman without a past, her life began at Old Orchard Beach, the day my grandfather chose her. We reconstructed her life like a puzzle, with bits of information gleaned over the years, strands of string we tied together. We figured out that my grandmother's mother threw her husband out of the house because he was a violent drunk, and that she returned to live in the family house with her father and his horde of kids. We figured out that after the death of her mother, my grandmother, her two sisters Jeanne and Réjeanne and the brother who later became a priest all left, burning the bridges with the other brothers we knew nothing about. Rumour had it that a battle over an inheritance was behind it all. People said there was more than meets the eye, things happened at night that could not be talked about during the day, the father drank, the mother was a battered woman, a marriage quickly solemnized to legitimize the five children who had been born long before, and at the end of the line a divorce to put a stop to the hell on earth that had gone on much too long.

When my mother understood that a grandmother was not meant to bring up her granddaughter, she packed her bags and changed cities. She found a little apartment in a tall building, one bedroom and a fold-out couch in the living room. My mother might not have kept me if she had been a model, an actress, or a law student, if she'd had plans to climb Kilimanjaro or discover a new vaccine. Once I was born, she called the little crook to tell him the news: "Hello, you have a daughter." Strange coincidence, he answered, he was just thinking about her, and he used the occasion to announce his upcoming departure from the New World and, if possible, the universe. No one saw him again. Silence on the other end of the line, a soldier missing in action.

Maybe he never actually left. Maybe he covered his tracks and began his life afresh, maybe closer than we thought, in the neighbours' backyard. Or maybe he forgot everything, the past became as airy as hashish smoke or the steam from a Turkish bath, a ghost in an old story he carried around inside, like a shell fragment.

The Village

One day, another man appeared at the skirt of my mother's forest, in a red Cortina that reminded me of those old Rolls-Royces in cartoons, black cars that make a terrible racket. He was a Prince Charming of his day, with a mustache and a lavender suit. This prince was the right one, the one who was going to stay.

He had come to annul the evil spell that had been cast six years earlier, a true-love kiss and the next day they were married. We left the little Rapunzel apartment perched at the top of the tower. We deserted the city and settled where they say the air is cleaner, life is better, and happiness gambols in the meadow. I packed my pink Cinderella suitcase and said farewell to the neighbour with the long blond hair. After a few hours of bouncing along the highway, spitting out black smoke, we found ourselves in the middle of a field that stretched as far as the eye could see, drenched in the heavy essence of manure.

Anjou, Ontario. That was the name of the village, a town hemmed in by cornfields and forest, where people spoke fractured French in a suburban décor. Something like a suburb, but too far from the big city to be a real suburb, and too ugly to be a real village. It was a new town, the way people claim that urban growths are actually cities, a town without centuries-old houses. It was a territory with no lakes or rivers or trees. A universe of rusty sheet metal, twisted aluminum, cracked concrete, plywood, linoleum, polyester, and shag carpets.

For convenience's sake, people called it the country. They said the country instead of banal. They said the country instead of crummy. They said the country instead of boring. They said the country instead of admitting to the perverts and crazy men in the fields along the highway. At the end of August, we bought baskets of corn and husked it on the porch or the kitchen counter. There was silk everywhere, even between our toes. My mother would put a little milk in the cooking water. At the table I watched her hold the burning-hot cob between her fingertips and roll it in the butter dish. She left a deep imprint in the butter, a kind of hoop, a cradle, like the tiny manger I would hold in the palm of my hand at Christmas when my mother set up the crèche at the foot of the tree. Baby Jesus was the cherry on the sundae.

Boundary Road. Across from the bungalow at the edge of the village where we lived, there were the neighbours, the door to the hell of rural life. They watched the evening news and nibbled on buttered popcorn cooked on the stove in a metal dish covered with aluminum foil that formed a canopy with the hot air and exploding kernels underneath. During the day, *Allô Police* was always lying open on the kitchen table, with the photos of victims, torn clothing, bloodstains, the chalk outline of a corpse. Every day they followed the announcements of missing girls. "Hear ye, hear ye, another one gone!" as if it were a trophy. They counted the victims the way dead soldiers are counted on the battlefield.

Those stories enfolded us, they comforted us, I figured one day one of those girls would come knocking at the door after running for hours through the darkness. She would be standing outside the door of our red brick and stucco bungalow. She would have no shoes on her feet, she wouldn't have a coat, her hair would be tangled, her face covered in soot like in Victor Hugo, she would be damaged, she would knock on the side door, the one we walked past when we went to the basement, that led to the car under its aluminum shelter. The girl would be frozen, her feet broken, we would open the door so she could get warm. My mother would take the phone and call her parents. "Yes, she's here, you don't need to worry, she's safe now." As she waited for them to come for her, the girl would stop being afraid. She would share my room, sleep on the floor next to me, and when she was better, we would fall asleep drawing pictures on each other's backs with our fingertips, try and guess, a flower, a sun, a house, the neighbour's dog. We would be twins in our matching pajamas. We would fall asleep whispering secrets to each other.

I thought about that in the evening, after agreeing to go to bed, teeth and toilet, kisses for my mother and my new father, sometimes a few guilty tears after misbehaving or asserting my personality a little too much, only my mother's forgiveness could help me vanquish the monsters that kept sleep away. Sometimes I would fall asleep thinking about the splitting headaches my mother complained of, crying over the thought that she might have cancer. I don't know what frightened me most, her death or my life continuing on without her. Maybe it wasn't one or the other, but the impossibility of absorbing her pain, the proof we really were separate.

In this life there were girls who disappeared, cancer, mushroom clouds that were born slowly but went on to fill the entire TV screen. At school, in the playground, within earshot of the monitors, a little girl told me that if the atomic bomb ever fell on us, the way the man on the news predicted, instead of running away, she was going to run right for its centre and be instantaneously pulverized. She made that clear. Her name was Paula because her father named her Paul and in the end they added an A. She repeated her resolution almost every day in the playground, and I didn't understand why she wanted to rush to destruction instead of letting it come to her since no one could escape it anyway. The hot line was the temperature of the cold war in everyday life. She said, "I'd rather die quick than be simmered in a pot over low heat, Mr. Wolf," and when I went to bed, I kept seeing these images parading past my eyes.

The close-ups of Elvis Presley in the pages of the gossip papers. It was the dog days, the burnt end of summer. The autopsy photos showed lungs blackened by smoke and full of holes, like pieces of rotten calf's liver displayed next to a heart too purple and too swollen. The neighbours kept saying, "It's a scandal" and shaking their heads over and over as if they'd lost their minds, their seven daughters poring over the papers alongside them, a few tears shed together for the King since they couldn't make it to Graceland.

Elvis was white and fat and puffy. On his night table, they found bottles filled with a fine collection of technicolour pills. "Look," they said to me, and I didn't know what I was supposed to see. The paper said it wasn't him, Elvis wasn't dead, he had met Nixon and they made him disappear into the witness protection program. A wax likeness had been laid in his coffin with a fan so it wouldn't melt, it practically weighed a ton. They said that despite everything, despite the alcohol, the meat, the drugs, Elvis couldn't weigh that much. People started looking for more proof and they found it in his middle name, Aaron, engraved on his gravestone by his father, and misspelled. The sign that the father knew that the son who was buried there wasn't the right one.

Then, with one last sigh, we learned that the book Elvis was reading on the toilet, a few fractions of a second before his death, was actually still at the printer's when he died. A book about the Shroud of Turin. That was proof that Elvis, like Jesus, wasn't dead. On the same page, a cheap advertisement urged us to buy autographed portraits of our favourite stars, a little like when my mother bought a Chinese kid at school for twenty-five cents. In exchange for five dollars, you could receive a unique, one-of-a-kind picture signed by the star's own hand, direct from Hollywood.

The neighbours' youngest daughter Manon-just-Manon said that since Elvis had signed his name, there was no way he was dead, the signature was a miracle from beyond the grave. Choosing Elvis got her congratulations and a pat on the head, like a dog when it fetches the prey. What I wanted more than anything else was the iron grip of the Bionic Woman, my Friday night television idol, her ordinary beauty and superhuman strength, long before she began shilling for Select Comfort mattresses at the end of her career. Jamie Sommers was beautiful, strong, and intelligent. She was tall and slender and had no breasts. A real heroine.

All the parents agreed, even my mother who openly made fun of it. "It's just a trap, a gimmick." But I begged and she gave in, and a few weeks later two Polaroids showed up, they had been sent from an address far to the north of the one we were expecting. They came from the biggest city in the area, far from the flash and glitter of

Hollywood, the paradise we dreamed of every night. The camera had been placed very close to a black and white television screen, and then click — we got gypped.

When she saw the photos, my mother smiled a knowing smile that said too much. I was mad at her for not sharing my hopes and for having been right all along. I was mad at her for not having had faith, the way I was mad at her on Sundays for letting me go to church alone and not being ashamed when Monday morning came around and the teacher asked, "Who didn't go to church yesterday?"

Every morning I passed by the neighbours' house before school. When the sun went down I returned there obediently to wait for my parents to get home. The neighbours lived in a fabulous split-level, with an enormous garage you could reach from the kitchen, full bathrooms, cozy bedrooms, a living room, kitchen, and dining room with a fixture of fake crystal hanging above the table made of dark fake wood, a finished basement covered in plywood, and at the far end of the yard, past the vegetables, goats, chickens, and the doghouse, was a shed as big as the Seven Dwarves' house. Further on, and behind, came the forest with its rabbit and snowmobile trails under the pines.

We girls went to school in a raggedy line. We waited at the railroad tracks, prisoners of the level crossing because a freight train decided to stop and block the way and make us late for marbles and dodge ball. The neighbour girls were used to it, they slipped under the cars like eels and kept going. I was afraid and waited for the train to start up again so a wheel wouldn't crush me and drag my body to some other village, cut, sliced, flattened like the pennies we put on the tracks so the train wheels would erase the Queen's face. I heard my mother's voice, her finger pointed at my nose, forbidding me from doing what the other girls did. I was more afraid of disobeying her than risking their pitiless contempt, sarcasm, and mockery. For them I'd always be the girl from somewhere else. I wasn't born here, they watched me show up on the horizon without being invited and it was already too late, I would never be part of the clan. The girls left me behind and went on their way. Once the train moved off and the coast was clear, I walked far behind and didn't try to catch up to them.

The road crossed the village from one end to the other, starting at our house, the last one, to the first, which had been turned into a credit union. Between the two extremities, besides the two hundred houses that punctuated the territory like exclamation marks, there was the elementary school, the church with the tall steeple, Chez Bouboule's French-fry stand, the corner store that sold Guy Lafleur hockey cards, and the community hall where the Knights of Columbus and the Cercle des fermières organized their fund-raisers.

The cars drove past at high speed. I was walking in the gravel and drawing circles with my feet. The sun turned stroboscopic as it hit the tall elms planted along the road. Whenever they could, the villagers told the story of the Beauregard twin sisters for the thousandth time. They died one after the other, one week apart, at the same time of day, driving on this road. They had both been struck by the rays of the sun that flashed and triggered in the first, then the second, an epileptic fit, the loss of control of their vehicle, the car wrapped around an electric pole, instant death.

From the road that was a little raised, I soon saw the playground come into view. In the winter, a big rink was set up where girls flirted with the hockey players until their feet froze. When spring returned, we played marbles and dodge ball, we had a game where we would throw a red, white, and blue ball against the wall, turn around twice, clap our hands five times, jump up and down, then catch the ball. Sometimes, on Saturdays and Sundays, when I was especially bored, I would walk across the village and go to the playground. There would be no one around except, sometimes, the former priest who, for lack of a better occupation, was now the principal, and he would appear out of nowhere dressed in black with a gold cross hanging around his neck. He had forgotten something, a list, a book, a file, the old brown leather strap he hung on a nail in his office, displayed in full view by the door. When the desire overcame him, he would take it down and, as he talked to the child facing him, he would nonchalantly play with it, like a knight with his sword.

The old men in the village would call him "Father" and obediently lower their eyes. I did all I could to stay out of his way.

My village was the kind of village where people were proud to say that everyone knew everyone else. It was a village like any other, like any other place where people keep watch and claim they love one another. It was that way, and sometimes worse than that. You had to work hard to protect a secret. You had to be skilled, and sneaky, you had your hands full. It was a little like carefully building the plot of a detective novel, and afterward, for weeks, you lived off the effort.

It was the kind of village you were better off forgetting, and even when you tried, you were haunted by the hot dog stand on the main street and the swimming pool at the campground that was stuck out by the exit to the highway, where the villagers streamed when July rolled around. Families left the grid of the centre of the village and set up shop one kilometre away, at Camp Kittawa, one next to the other in tents and trailers, they spent their weeks' vacation there and of course every weekend, from Friday evening to Sunday.

The campground lay at the edge of Larose's woods. The wealthy people could afford spots by the pool and the road, and the poor pitched their tents in the middle of the forest, on the carpet of needles dropped by the tall pine trees. The ground smelled of humus and ferns. After it rained, when the sun brought steam rising out of the earth, a vague smell of excrement hung in the air, and underneath it the scent of chlorine from the pool, and vinegar from the bags of Yum-Yum chips they sold at the gate, in the little shelter, along with the tent-car-barbe-cue packages and wads of Hubba Bubba bubblegum that didn't stick. When luck smiled upon us, a bag of chips would have a coupon in it that gave us a second bag free and that bag had a coupon in it too for another free bag and that went on till our bellies were stuffed and the sun went down. The chips were thin and fragile and greasy. One bite and they fell apart in your mouth. The vinegar stung your tongue and made the inside of your cheeks tingle.

As the summer days went by with the chlorine treat-ments, the skin of my nose would peel off in slices, worn-out skin that I pulled off, underneath was the pale pink of fresh flesh. We would forget the sunscreen and our hats. For the duration of the summer, the children turned into crustaceans forced head first, their arms flapping, into boiling water. My stained face was discoloured, like an old car whose doors had been eaten away by rust.

Between sessions at the local campground, the villagers religiously looked after their livestock. It was an obligation, a sign of belonging to rural life, the way you made sure of your identity by reading the horoscope on the last page of the paper. Ours was the sign of the rabbit. We had gotten a pair from a local farmer and they were quietly munching away in the yard. We adopted them as a community gesture. The female had white fur with black spots, and the male was black with white spots. They sported Hitler and Charlie Chaplin mustaches. We didn't know anything about animals, but we were ready to follow instructions.

We set up the rabbit hutch in the yard behind the bungalow. The cages leaned against the wall under my bedroom window. At night I could hear the metal rocking. Not long after, babies were born, and we took care of them when they were sick, and petted them because they were as soft as silk, we let them run free in the grass and hoped that like dogs they would come sprinting back to us if we snapped our fingers or would know how to find us if we got lost in a snowstorm and were freezing to death. They lived there a while, long enough to fill up one cage, then two cages, then three, six, long enough for my parents to say that rabbits were coming out of their ears, they'd have to find a solution, what were we thinking of?

I heard everything but understood nothing, certainly not the reference to the neighbour's friend who was an expert in this kind of problem, nor my mother's comment about trying chickens next time. One morning, I went to feed the animals as I did every morning. "You should do your bit, it'll be your job." I discovered that all the cages were empty, all except one, the one in the middle, at the back was mound of red meat, formless and bloody, a sticky piece of play-dough where I could see the delicate slits of little closed faces and aborted ears. I opened my eyes wide, then closed them, and opened them again and rubbed them to be sure I had seen what I had seen, a pile of dead baby bunnies, absolutely tiny, all together in a heap, little babies that had been killed. From the pile of bodies, the oldest ones had been taken to make pâté, and in the struggle, the newborns had been forgotten and, just as she was caught in the snare, one of the young females had given birth, out of fear. Later that's what they told me as if it were the most normal thing in the world, you can give birth out of terror too, the mother and the children and everyone else ends up in the pot, life has nothing more to do with it.

Either the act had already been done, and the babies already born, but since crimes are committed in the dark, no one had thought to check if any of the young were left behind when they took the mother. Or they knew, and didn't care. I stood there, frozen, in front of the hutch like in a Saturday morning cartoon, when the characters have their eyelids held open wide by toothpicks. I ran inside to call my mother. But life in the village and work in the big city are in different time zones, and I couldn't speak to her.

I never found out if the babies were born and died shortly after, or if everything happened to them at once, light and darkness both. Between my body and theirs, there wasn't a barrier but a mirror, like at the beauty shop or the tavern, on the back wall above the bar. There was a mess of organs, insides and outsides all together, the pale pink of gums or a little girl's vagina when you unfold it like a book. In a ball, a heap, it looked like snails, a length of intestine, a turtle's neck.

No one said what they did with the newborns to dispose of them, where they had been put, in the big green plastic can where we threw dead leaves and garbage, or in the white kitchen bag under the sink.

The neighbours across the way always wore soft white or brown or grey rabbit's feet on their jeans, or hung them on their key-chains. The neighbours said the dead foot of a dead rabbit brought good luck. The rabbit's fur was like down or cotton, and it was in fashion. It covered wallets, handbags, and those sexy little jackets worn with jeans so tight the zipper had to be pulled up with a hanger and you had to suck in your stomach until it touched your backbone. People made pompons out of the fur to decorate their winter boots.

It was dark, it was snowing hard, the red Cortina was frozen, and it protested against having to run in weather like this. But midnight mass was sacred. If you didn't go, it was like thumbing your nose at the whole village. On the church steps, after the ceremony, the parishioners shook hands and laughed, happy knowing they would soon be set free for the annual bout of drunkenness consecrated by the Good Lord. Impatient children pulled on their parents' jackets, there were pretty packages waiting, the fine, shiny paper waiting under the tree that had been cut this morning, Larose's woods had the very best ones. The women compared their midnight supper menus, and the cost of what they had bought, the roast beef on special or the ham, and how the Yule log was always too expensive. The men smoked one last cigarette and urged each other on with a slap on the back, the whisky went from hand to hand like liquid courage. Then, one by one, the families went their separate ways. In single file, the cars left the centre of the village for the four points of the compass in the festive play of headlights that must have made the Good Lord proud. Seen from the sky, it must have looked like a star.

Since we were outsiders, the neighbours imagined that the guests at our midnight supper must have come from far away, the other end of the 417, or further still, further than how long it took to listen to both sides of a Joe Dassin tape, maybe as far as the ocean but they didn't really know. They figured our guests came from the old world, they were rich snobs, people who used flowery words that no one really understood when they came out of their mouths.

Once, during Christmas vacation, the neighbours went away alone for a weekend in New York. It was the trip of a lifetime, a second honeymoon they bit into in the big American apple. They flitted off like two lovebirds, a role they had learned from a thick document supplied by the priest. When they returned, proud of their adventure, they stuck a bumper sticker on the car: WWME. They had taken the World Wide Marriage Encounter course. Soon, we could see them walking hand in hand through the centre of the village, then turn back toward the house, a brief moment in front of the presbytery, kisses complete with tongues and big hugs. They were the local poster boy and girl for marital harmony.

As the years went by, after their wedding at age eighteen, they filled their house with seven girls, following the parish priest's recommendations about letting divine grace flow in the missionary position, either that or putting an aspirin between your knees. And so were born Nathalie, Josée, Isabelle, Carole, Chantal, Lyne, right down to Manon-just-Manon, the little afterthought whose survival was never a sure thing because Mom was too old the day before she was conceived. He had a construction business, and they called him Daddy. When he came back from a job site, he sat down at the end of the table, emptied his plate without a word, and settled in front of the television, saying, "I need to relax." The girls had to be quiet and go out into the yard, play with the garden dwarves, smoke hay, and make rabbit-raisin sandwiches.

When the girls were at school, Mom spent the quiet afternoons in the living room, reclining on the ochre sofa covered with giant brown and violet flowers, set on legs sculpted into lion's feet. Above her, on the wall, was a portrait of Elvis on black velvet framed in fake baroque gilt, back when he was young and handsome. Protected by the king of rock and roll, she would lie back with her gossip magazines, reading and drinking litres of Kool-Aid and rum and Coke. That was her secret garden.

A few hours later, the family would find her busy in the kitchen, making pies with cherry filling that tasted like jelly beans. She would make nun's farts with the leftover dough and prepare the evening meal, chicken gizzards and gluey, flat dumplings in thick gravy. At noon she'd served fluorescent orange Kraft Dinner with peeled cucumbers cut into hockey pucks and crowned with a spoonful of Cheez Whiz. At the end of the day, when her eldest daughter came back from school, she would squeeze the pimples that blossomed on her forehead. She worked carefully, sticking out the tip of her tongue, the way she did when she sewed costumes for Hallowe'en and satin dresses for the senior prom. The entire village marvelled at her work, they said she had magic fingers, they could have just as well said her fingers were boney and crooked like the talons of a vulture or the claws of an old witch who fattens up children before roasting them in the oven.

Manon-just-Manon was my age and had dark eyes and black bangs that fell flat on her forehead. She looked like she came from the great north, from an Innu reserve. If her mother hadn't been who she was, plump and pious, people would have figured Manon-just-Manon was a spare part, the daughter of the guy who delivered *Le Droit* every afternoon because he couldn't get up in the morning. Manon-just-Manon didn't look like anyone, and people said, "She's not a girl, she's a boy."

In the summer she would come knocking on the door, at mealtime, and ask me to go pick strawberries with her in the field across the way. My mother sighed and told her I had to finish eating first, so she would go and sit on the porch steps to wait, glancing furtively toward the dining room, curious to see what was on our plates. In winter we would skate together on the frozen ditches along Boundary Road with a piece of wood in our hands for a hockey stick. When it wasn't too cold, we would make castles by crushing the snow into shapes with our feet. We set up walls, we built furniture, we made up stories, we forgot we were girls. Manon-just-Manon became the head of the family.

The moon was full. It shone brightly in the sky above our heads, aquamarine the way I imagined the depths of the sea would be. The air was pure. We lay down in the snow and pretended to sleep, and stayed there until the cold made pins and needles run up our hands and feet. The evening turned to darkness, and soon we heard a voice calling that it was time to come inside, and we would get up from the ground slowly, leaning against each other. We emerged from the snow like from a bath full of hot water, numb, slowed, almost paralyzed.

One autumn morning before school, Manon-just-Manon came into the kitchen of her house holding a little cat. The kitten was completely stiff, with its four paws sticking out straight. Its yellow eyes were wide open. Her mother glanced in her direction, and without interrupting the Jell-O she was making for lunch, told her, "It's dead! Get it out of here right now!" Manon-just-Manon answered, "No, he's just frozen, I'm going to warm him up." She went into her room and came back with the kitten in her arms, wrapped in a doll's blanket. She held the animal tight against her stomach. Attracted by the noise, her sisters came to have a look before rushing off to smear mascara on their eyelashes, as her mother kept muttering, "Good thing your father's not here." I hovered next to her, my heart beating, maybe the Baby Jesus would return as the cat's ninth life.

After fifteen minutes or so, one paw started to move, then another, then a third, then the light returned to its yellow eyes and Manon-just-Manon let out a cry. "Look, Mom, he's alive!" Her mother, who was busy slicing the crust off Paris Pâté sandwiches, turned and gave her daughter a quick look, then went back to cutting crusts, but the next time she came back she had one eyebrow raised. It was a mystery, no one could say if it was God or the Devil, but the kitten had come back to life. Manon-just-Manon had been right, she must have had a gift, Mom was going to have a word with the priest about it.

But in the meantime, she wasn't changing her position. "Get it out of my kitchen, you can leave it in the garage but not the living room." I followed Manon-just-Manon into her room, and she asked me to take the little doll's bed with the pink and white mattress, we were going to put it in the garage, a nursery for a resuscitated cat. Neither of us knew if it was a boy cat or a girl cat, and where to look to find out. Manon-just-Manon said, "We'll say it's a girl, and we'll call her Barbie." I said, "Okay" because there was no arguing allowed, with me she always decided everything, especially since her parents had gone to the WWME, and the younger daughters went to sleep at their uncle's who raised cows and pigs. Manon-just-Manon hadn't talked about it, she had gathered warm eggs freshly shat out of the hens, and drunk litres of milk that was too fatty and fresh. Now, when her mother set the pint on the table in front of her, Manon-just-Manon didn't say anything, but her face turned whiter than the milk, and her eyes darker still, her whole body retreated. She lowered her head and didn't look at me, and I did the same, like at mass, like a prayer.

The kitten stayed in the garage the rest of the day. When we got back from school, it wasn't there. Manon-just-Manon ran into the kitchen, shouting, "Mom, where's Barbie?" I don't know what Mom said. From where I was, there were no words in the screams. Daddy had come back from the job. He was sitting in front of the TV. There was a funny smell in the house, the smell of something wet, dirty, and a little sweet. That evening, Manon-just-Manon didn't come out to play. I sat on the steps between the garage and the family room. When my parents got home, I crossed the street fast and went inside.

When Manon-just-Manon got sick of me, she would yell a string of insults, anything as long as the arrow hit the heart of the apple balanced on my head. Proud of her aim, she would head back to her house as if freed of some weight, a few dance steps, angel's wings, her feet hitting the fresh asphalt. That's what having neighbours meant. The next day, she was back like nothing ever happened.

One Saturday, at the end of the afternoon, we met a boy who lived at the corner, right by the railroad tracks. When we were bored stiff, we'd play with him. He lived alone with his mother, who used to be a loose woman, in a house with an enormous chandelier hanging from the ceiling. Sometimes a piece fell off, an elongated tear of polished glass, and I picked it up on the sly and gave it to my mother. I told her, "Look at the pretty diamond! I found it for you!" She made an ugly face and answered, "That's no treasure, you might as well throw it out."

The boy was filthy, and his name was Marcel. He wasn't all there, a little slower than how the world turned. He had hair to his shoulders, and always tangled like a fisherman's line, with caterpillar cocoons and spider webs in it. He spent all day in his mother's store that she'd set up in the basement after the end of her first career. A sign stood in the yard in front of the house: *A Woman's Heart. Inti-*

mate *Apparel and Fabrics*. Once Manon-just-Manon spotted Marcel playing with a dog in another yard, and she said to me, "Come on, let's go see Filthy Boy, he's with the dog." I followed and didn't say anything. We went around the back to surprise him. We crept past the cedar hedge that separated the house from the neighbour's who owned the dog, a really nasty German shepherd that had been excluded from civilization by a sign that read *Cave Canem*. That meant *Cavern Dog*; we knew how to read.

When he caught sight of us, Marcel didn't say anything, he went on waving a stick above the dog's head to make it jump and show its rabid, foaming fangs. Manon-just-Manon asked, "What are you doing?" Marcel didn't answer. "You want to play with us?" Marcel the Filthy Boy stared at her, threw the stick over the other side of the hedge as the German shepherd looked on in disbelief, then he said, "Okay." For a second or two, no one moved. We didn't know what we wanted to do. Then Manon-just-Manon showed the way. We followed her to a wooden shed at the back of Marcel's yard, an old rundown shelter where a few rusty shovels and rakes were hanging. There, since we didn't have any better ideas, we played Pants Down. Manon-just-Manon looked at Marcel and said, "You go first." We didn't have to ask twice, he slipped his thumbs under the elastic of his shorts and pulled. He wasn't wearing underwear, just a squished-up little shrimp. He stood there with his pants down, and we waited for something to happen too, as if suddenly the world was going to change.

Manon-just-Manon's face got all sour. She lifted her eyes to the sky, and like a corporal ready for battle, she issued her last judgement: "This game is stupid." She motioned me to follow and we ran off. We left Marcel the Filthy standing there and went into the strawberry field to try and find the brown garter snake that we called Claudette. Manon-just-Manon told me, "If we find her, then we'll have some fun."

For my eighth birthday, I got a chocolate cake in the shape of a cat. We blew out the candles, sang a song and, after the celebration, they told me I had reached the age of reason like kids in China who are sent to work in the factories. I came back from school with a string around my neck and a key hanging from the end of it. In winter, night fell early. As my parents drove back from work, I sat in the darkness of the living room. I did the breakfast dishes, then turned on the television to have a presence in the house, and Charlie's Angels, those celestial creatures, would appear.

One evening, it wasn't late, the side doorbell rang. It was after school, the sun had set, the man was wearing a fireman's costume. He wasn't part of the village volunteer department – I'd seen them when our class did a project on jobs and professions. He said, "I'm an inspector," and pointed to the badge on his chest and the stripes on his shoulders. He said he came from the next village, the one that has a restaurant where they serve pizza and Chinese rolls covered in sticky brown sauce that's supposed to come from plums.

He wanted to know if my parents were home, he wanted to talk to them. I looked through the holes in the lace and asked, "Who is it?" like in the Three Little Pigs. I didn't know if I should open the door. I figured he was an adult, after all, and besides he was a man with a shiny broach and a uniform. I don't remember when he decided to leave, how long he stayed, what colour the sky was. I don't remember what he said. Maybe he checked the smoke detectors, there's one above the stairs, and another when you go into the living room. "Don't forget to change the batteries." I just remember he talked the whole time as I jumped up and down on one leg and then the other to get a look at the TV screen where that beautiful Farah Fawcett was fighting the bad guys with her long wavy hair that all the girls tried to imitate with their curling irons. That evening, Farah Fawcett had to find a missing beauty queen. In the megaphone, Charlie's deep voice said, "We have to hurry before it's too late." At the end of the show, with a great kick, the Angels knocked down the door to a motel room where the girl was, sitting on the bed in her gown, as fresh as a flower, everything was fine, nothing had happened to her. The next thing we knew, she was on stage, adjusting the crown they had placed on her head, with an enormous bouquet of flowers in her arms. She had won first prize, and standing in the wings were Charlie's Angels, applauding.

The fireman went away and left behind some brochures on home safety. He went away and I didn't even notice. Sitting in front of the TV, I had forgotten all about him.

Night fell in the picture window. I recognized the shape of the red Cortina that slowed as it came up to the house. I watched how it turned into the driveway. I listened to the sound of the tires crunching over the gravel and the motor that let out a final shudder once the ignition was turned off. The doors slammed one after the other in their aluminum frames. There were paper bags rustling, the sound of voices, and my parents coming up the steps with their arms loaded with provisions for the week and as a special treat a bucket of Kentucky fried chicken. I turned off the television. My mother put the grease-stained boxes on the table with the plastic forks and plates. We waited for the bags to be emptied, and the food put away, then we sat down around the mountain of chicken in its shiny robe of breading as if it were a campfire. We passed around the box filled with fries and the Styrofoam containers with their heaps of coleslaw and macaroni as if they were a peace pipe. I only liked the white meat with its crispy, salty skin, and the elbow macaroni that stung my tongue because of the little green dots in the white sauce that might have been an exotic spice or the product of the latest chemical innovation. With the day's work and the long commute on her face, you would have thought my mother was sad if you didn't know how tired she was because of everything she had to do to be a modern woman. Once she had to spend three weeks in bed because of a nasty case of pneumonia. I don't know how we managed to survive. Years later, her ladies' operation took her away from us again for a few days, a free vacation at the hospital in exchange for being eviscerated. When she returned, she could hardly walk, she spent all day in her nightgown, lying on the sofa, holding her stomach. That's where she would be when I came back from school, stretched out on the white sofa in the late afternoon sunlight. I had grown up, I borrowed her jewelry, her shoes, her flowered dresses to forget that there was still distance between us.

The girl who lived in the house that stood right next to our bungalow, on the same side of Boundary Road, the girl who was my other neighbour, her name was BB. She lived with her parents and her little brother in a white trailer, and next to it there was another one just like it where her aunt and uncle lived. We hardly ever saw them, they did business overseas, and when they were around, it was never for very long. People said they went back and forth between the village and the United States, they went to New York all the time, the city that everyone in the village talked about because you had to go there at least once in your life. People said they had a business though they never said what they sold or bought or sold again. I only knew that when they came back, BB's mother would get very upset. Usually she let her kids play outside until late after dark without even calling them for supper, but suddenly she was very impatient to get dinner in them. She stood in the little strip of land between our houses and screamed her lungs out. "You stinky little bastards, get your asses in the house right now before I grab you by the ear and drag you in!"

BB was named after Brigitte Bardot, her mother's idol. Her mother stapled enormous, full-length portraits of her on the plywood living room walls. She swore by her

Dairy Queen hair-do and imagined she was the impossible dream of every married man, a scandal, a mermaid, a miracle, a cake slathered in whipped cream. BB was alone a lot of the time. She looked after her little brother and waited for her parents to come back from work – her mother was an exotic dancer at a truck stop on the 417 and her father delivered toilet paper. Plenty of times she left her little brother alone in the big field out back and pedalled her bike to Serge the Hunk's place where he was waiting for her.

Sometimes, on Fridays, the parents came to school early to pick up the kids. They would go out that evening and not come back till the next afternoon, they left BB and her brother with an old lady in the neighbourhood who looked after children to make ends meet. When they showed up at school to get their kids, the better to get rid of them afterward, they would be wearing their red and black satin jackets that made them look like a bowling team or Donny and Marie's backup singers. They were tall and slender and always touching each other, their long legs wrapped in tight jeans, their hair sticky with lacquer. Standing next to her parents, with her dark skin, her curly hair, and her little round belly, BB looked like an accident.

One afternoon, BB practically ran out of school when the bell rang because we had to take advantage of our freedom. She invited me to her place until her parents came back. Her brother was digging holes out in front of the house, dozens, hundreds of holes to catch wolves or maybe snakes. BB told him that wolves don't hide in holes. He gave her a dirty look and answered, "You don't know anything!" and she said, "You're too stupid" and turned her back on him. Her little brother stayed outside and dug holes and BB took my hand and opened the aluminum door of the trailer.

She had the room at the back with a high window and a red chenille bedspread. On her bedside table, there was a dish full of bits of pink licorice and candies. She picked up a handful and sat cross-legged on the bed, her skirt high on her thighs, her white cotton underpants had flowers on them. My mother was always telling me, "Pull your skirt down over your knees! Sit straight and pay attention to your clothes!" Standing in the doorway I watched BB who had started rocking back and forth on her mattress with a book in her hand, a little book that was fat and soft, a book without pictures like the ones adults read. She said, "My aunt gave it to me the last time she was here, you should come and see, she told me there's nothing better

41

than this book to teach you everything you should know."

Sitting on the bed, she handed me the book. My eyes fastened on the woman with the very pale skin who took up the middle of the cover, her lips were half open, she was lying back wearing a tight, fire-red dress that clung to her waist and had a plunging neckline. Her dress was pushed high up on her legs like BB's skirt, white thighs wide open. A giant man was standing behind her. It looked like she was about to fall asleep, and he had caught her first. He was a Casanova with shiny hair and a brown, muscled chest. He was hiding his mocking smile under his thin mustache, and holding the woman's hair in his fist, pulling her head back. I didn't know if she was sleeping or if she was crying or if she was whimpering because it hurt. And I didn't understand why he was laughing.

Then BB grabbed the book out of my hands. She opened it and picked a page, any page, and started reading out loud, stumbling over some of the sentences because reading wasn't her strong point. I listened to her, and blurry pictures started appearing behind my eyes, the scenes had nothing to do with the Time-Life book about sexuality that my mother bought so she wouldn't have to keep explaining how babies are made. BB was talking another language, she had a different voice, like the man who put on a show in the school gym. He made his dummy talk without moving his lips. He was the father of one of the girls in my class. During the whole show, she sat next to the teacher and didn't look up once at what her father was doing.

BB changed places. Now she was sitting on the edge of the bed, right close to me. She said, "That's real life, with that you understand everything, it's a hundred times better than biology class!"

Another time, when her brother was trying to dig holes in the linoleum floor in the kitchen, and she was fed up hearing him banging away, BB came over to my house to eat soda crackers. She sat on the kitchen counter and talked on and on, and a storm of white crumbs rained down on her. Nothing could stop her. The sentences ran on, words, stories, stuff she had heard or invented. BB talked like a machine gun, her mouth was a junkyard. In it she kept the story of a little girl who took a rusty potato peeler from the kitchen drawer without her mother finding out, and cut through the door that closes off girls' bodies. I didn't understand a thing. It was a guessing game like the one the inspector in the fireman's costume played. BB said the word *door* and I thought, "Open, Sesame!" I pictured the set of little red knives my mother used to make our food and my teeth clenched, my forehead grew wrinkles of horror, my head started spinning. BB went on telling her story, on and on, the crumbs accumulated around her, I didn't say anything, the peanut butter stuck to the roof of my mouth, pretty soon we'd be buried.

I didn't know if BB was telling the truth or if it was a rumour or an example someone had given her of what you had to do in life. If it was the destiny of little girls who grow up in trailers at the edge of a hay field where garter snakes crawl on their bellies without a sound. It certainly had nothing to do with the Jeannettes my mother took me to once a week, at the community centre. All the girls who were old enough to be signed up were there.

The meetings happened after the evening meal, a break from taking a bath or doing your homework. The girls in my class were there, BB and Manon-just-Manon, each of us metamorphosed by the polyester skirts and the sky-blue blouses, our devoted faces set off by the yellow cotton tie whose knot no one could make exactly right. When we came in, the group leaders had us sit in a circle on the freshly washed floor. On the first meeting, we received a treasure: in our hands they placed a copy of the girl's guide to being a good Jeannette, the precious notebook that everyone had to have with prayers, songs, fables, and a white page for writing congratulations. Months later, mine still didn't have anything written in it. I figured I'd never be a chief even if I followed every path perfectly, and carefully picked the *live with courage and strength* blue flower, the *be honest and trustworthy* white one, and the *share in the sisterhood of Guiding* golden one.

As soon as spring came, I began dreading my inevitable stay at Lake Green in the dead of summer, sleeping in barracks with a common shower, the clearings somewhere in the middle of the woods, the campfires where the leaders made us accept the hard truths about ourselves and used the opportunity to drive us to tears. The next day, they walked slowly during the hike, in the hot noontime sun that gave you a headache, unsteady on their thighs riddled with cellulite, proudly brandishing a banner high in the sky as we brought up the rear, panting for breath. We knew that when evening came, there wouldn't be marshmallows for grilling at the end of a stick over the campfire because they made you fat. At Lake Green, we traded in our skirts for a pair of shorts and a T-shirt, its blue the equivalent for girls of the black the nuns wore. Instead of a tie we got a handkerchief that we'd fold diagonally and wrap around our necks. My two poles were fear and boredom, the desire to be alone and the fear of isolation. Going home was a relief, the feeling, once a week, that I'd earned my ticket to heaven by performing a good deed, which was doing something I hated.

Meetings among the Jeannettes began with sitting in a circle holding hands and reciting an ode to the Virgin Mary. Then they told us the true story of Jeannette who reminded you a little of Maria Goretti, who died at eleven, and all the other woman saints who became saints because they refused, thanks to God, the advances of mortal men and turned to the body of Christ and kept it stuck in their throat. That didn't change anything when it came to the men who wanted to rape them, but when they were killed for having resisted with a prayer on their lips, we were told how admirable they were, the way they swore off earthly pleasures, power, and wealth, to seek their reward in heaven. That was the story of Saint Martina, patron saint of Rome, an orphan who had inherited riches from her parents. She was scourged and her flesh torn with iron hooks and nails, potsherds, and sharp swords, she was scalded with boiling oil, condemned to be devoured by wild beasts in the amphitheatre, thrown on a burning pile from which she escaped unhurt. Some of the men who had inflicted these tortures embraced the Christian faith. Like the voices Jeannette heard, a voice called Martina up to heaven. The earth shook, thunder rolled, and the temples dedicated to false gods collapsed.

Jeannette was Joan of Arc before wars and the stake, and she was the example to follow. There were Barbies, and there were girls who heard voices. At night, in bed, under the covers, I crossed my hands and made an effort, a little one, because you needed will to have faith. My grandmother gave me a rosary in a round gilt box with Byzantine designs. I liked to run the cold pearls between my fingers, one after the other, until I reached the tiny naked Christ on the cross. I lost my way in the numbers. I forgot the prayer I had just said. I spoke the words mechanically as I escaped toward other worlds. Then I replaced the pearls in their box and closed the cover tight as if there was a genie inside and it was a story from Aladdin.

For two years in that cursed village, my best friend was Valence Berri. We swore never to forget each other, come what may. For me, a name like hers was the very sound of hope. There weren't any other girls called Valence Berri. Her name came from geography class and Michelangelo paintings. She moved here from the big city with her parents. Her father was an insurance salesman and he visited all the villages in the county. He was rarely at home, a family dinner on Saturday evening, suit and tie for Sunday mass. Her mother was tall, blond, and gentle, and she ran her house like a summer camp. Valence was the oldest girl. After her, five more bodies came out of her mother's belly.

Not long after my tenth birthday, she dropped me. We had celebrated my birthday in the city, around the heated grill of a Japanese restaurant where the chef fried too many vegetables and little bits of meat that you really couldn't tell what it was. Suddenly, in front of the paper umbrellas, I became too small for her. Like flowers that lose their petals, playtime was over. Everything began to bore her, except the adult world that Philippe the Cute was urging her into, while I held her back in the world of dolls and make-believe. Valence Berri began to look through me. Her eyes were looking over to the other side.

Overnight, she got as tall as my mother. Adults praised her beauty, her pale blue eyes, her long blond hair. She started going out with Philippe, the village tough guy, a dark-haired boy all the girls admired from a distance because at recess, behind the trailer where the second grade classroom was set up, he would French kiss with Valence Berri and slide his hands under her AC/DC sweat shirt. Saturday afternoon, they'd go roller skating in Varsity, a village nearby where the mayor had decided to take a chance on building a roller derby track with grandstands and a canteen where you could eat the best all-dressed steamies in the world. It was the area hot spot, where our stars would hang out: Gérard Letarte, the Elvis imitator who'd won tons of prizes in Las Vegas, and Big Lucie who took to the track in minuscule pink satin shorts, with her flesh spreading in waves of fat from underneath.

But from then on, no matter where I came across her, Valence Berri immediately disappeared from my sight. She would not listen to my complaint. Her mother was ill at ease, she gave me pitying looks that said, "I can't do anything about it." How can you explain to someone that love isn't always requited? My mother told me, "You'll just have to get over it." I made myself imagine that Valence really had disappeared, she was gone, she'd evaporated into thin air, an ogre had kidnapped her.

For weeks, every night, I cried myself to sleep, picturing the only thing I was able to save, the memory of her face like a composite sketch stapled to a telephone pole.

On Saturday nights, we had parties in the half-finished basements of the bungalows, no adults allowed downstairs in the darkness to spy on us. Most of the time they used the opportunity to take off, digging a hole in the sand and sticking their parental heads in it, anyway, what's done is done, why would they pretend to be interested in us now? We immersed ourselves in the sound of electric guitars, the volume turned up full to make the whole world vibrate, starting with us, moved from within by the thrill that told us that happiness could exist. The high point of the evening was *Stairway to Heaven*, the longest slow dance in history. Once, the cousin or the brother of a girlfriend of mine got his mitts on me and pressed me tightly against him, with his long hands flattening my ass, and he didn't let go until the last note sounded.

After dancing in the dark, we turned on the lights and sat in a circle on the floor, then we spun an empty bottle to see who the neck would point to. Everyone waited for the game, it was the highlight of the evening along with the pretzels, peanuts, and barbecue chips. You could have heard a pin drop. When the bottle stopped, we followed the rules: the person who spun the bottle had to hide in the closet with the person the bottle pointed to. Our palms got wet, our hearts beat fast. Sometimes, if the bottle looked like it was going to stop in front of you, you jumped up, suddenly you had to go to the bathroom. When the two victims disappeared into the closet, we counted the minutes and kept our eyes on the clock on the wall, tick-tock, tick-tock, tick-tock, until the allotted time was over. We laughed, we whispered, the rumour factory was working at top speed. We didn't know if what happened behind the door was the same for everyone. We figured some people were more advanced than we were, and when they came out with rosy cheeks, we were sure they had actually exchanged their liquids and declarations of love.

Valence went into the closet with Philippe the Cute, and they stayed there longer than they had to. We watched the hands of the clock, we waited, finally we had to knock at the door, "Okay, okay, you can come out now." When he stepped out, Philippe puffed out his chest and buckled his belt. Valence's lips were red and her cheeks were white as if she'd swallowed a piece of apple sideways or was waiting for a real kiss. For a split second, our eyes met and the ghost of something passed between us, a fallen angel maybe, whatever it was, she wanted to bury it.

Once I ended up in the closet with Manon-just-Manon. I figured that was all right because we were neighbours. They say that all cats are grey in the dark, and in there I couldn't see a thing. I felt her hands on my shoulders, her mouth against my ear, and the secrets that ran sweetly down my cheek. In the dark, Manon-just-Manon was always nice.

That became clear during the end-of-year trip, on the way home, both of us curled up together on the last seat

51

at the back of the bus. For months, we'd had car washes in front of the fire station and gone door to door in the evening after school selling chocolate bars. All that to pay for a trip to Toronto, two nights and three days sleeping in a gym to see the CN Tower and celebrate the end of grade school and the graduation to the enormous concrete bunker that the Ministry of Education had constructed by the side of the highway, in the Bermuda Triangle formed by the other villages.

Montreal, the big city at the other end of the high-way, two hours from the village, had nothing in common with New York, the sparkling black jewel of our geography class, the teacher pointing it out on the map like the devil in the church basement in catechism class. New York was hell on earth, the residence of pestilence. Its gigantic ivory towers pointed to the sky in what was described as the arrogance of power, the certainty that the world was spread out at its feet. We said New York and saw the Statue of Liberty appear, and in the classroom a heavy silence settled in like at church on Sunday when one of the faithful had just died and the pitiful parishioners lowered their heads, no one dared look at the priest for fear he could see the colour of their souls through their eyes.

It was the summer of 1980. Not long after Joe Dassin's death came the announcement that Princess Caroline of Monaco and Philippe Junot were getting divorced. We felt there was some abstract link between these two events, something supernatural borne by the divine voice of *Paris Match*. Baby Azaria had disappeared from a campground in Australia, no one wanted to believe that the baby had been carried off by wild dogs, so the mother was accused.

School was over, and I lived in the heat of hay and mosquito bites. My mother complained about a referendum, then brightened up when an actor became a candidate for the presidency of the United States, and when we decided to boycott the Moscow Games, since everything was a mess everywhere. She spread out the brochures on the kitchen table, and sung the praises of horseback riding, sailing classes, mountain climbing, but I shook my head and categorically refused her idea, no matter how high quality the campers were said to be. I told her, "The problem isn't leaving here, it's being with other people and having to sleep, eat, wash, play, and talk with them, all the time, rain or shine." She said I was a hopeless case.

I remembered the summer of 1976, that summer of perfection, the Olympic Games on television, Nadia Comaneci's perfect 10s, the whole world watched in amazement, the contortions of that small body, her little ponytail held in place by a soft cloud of cloth, the arc of her back, she was like a feather, an angel. Soon we missed the little girl with the dark eyes on the beam in *Newsweek*.

Then the wonderment was over, even though the little gymnast had forced the judges to change the way they scored, soon people were saying she was anorexic, her life was miserable, her trainer had abused her. She was stripped bare in public and burned for sorcery. They said she was passed from man to man, from one fascism to the next, from Romania to the United States via Austria, the way she flew between the uneven bars. It was painful to see how she had been exiled from childhood, it was worse than leaving a country. They gave her medals so she would stay a little girl, so people could go on feeling butterflies in their stomach, and want to take her in their arms and feel her feline grace, to keep her within, like a Russian doll, a little marzipan girl. They built a nest of gossip for her since they couldn't pin her to a piece of velvet.

I stuck photos of Nadia Comaneci on my bedroom wall next to Farah Fawcett. When we went to Montreal to visit my grandparents, I looked for the stadium tower that points to the sky like an homage to the greatest girl on earth.

I was born just after Expo 67, where my mother worked as a cashier. People said my father worked there too for a few days, or a few hours maybe. I missed the whole thing. All I had was visiting the site with my grandparents years later on Sunday afternoons to have a picnic. That was one of their favourite things.

We would take the subway. We followed the arrow toward Man and His World to the end of the tunnel, with that smell that was always the same, a mix of metal and moisture, the coolness of it a welcome break after the heavy heat of the summer. When we reached the site, we would find a bench to sit and eat the little triangle-shaped sandwiches and the cucumber slices wrapped in wax paper. Sometimes, if we were lucky, we got to eat the meringues that always broke during the trip. Jeanne and Réjeanne, the great-aunts of my childhood, had made them, they had sacrificed their lives to take care of their mother at that crucial age when it's now or never because afterwards, when it comes to love, the handsome, strapping princes, you can forget about them. The idea of the meringues was better than the reality, a sticky thing that got into the spaces between your teeth and left a sugary taste of too much vanilla that ended up making you nauseous.

The great-aunts never came to the village. I saw them in Montreal, in their apartment decorated with their collection of porcelain statuettes of princesses, dancers, pastel-coloured courtesans, set out everywhere you looked on the white lacquered furniture, like the leftovers of childhood innocence. My grandfather made fun of them and whispered that they were collecting prostitutes, pornography for prudish old English ladies like the ones who served them when they went to make their purchases on the West Island, which was the activity that gave meaning to their existence. They had always lived together. They slept in twin beds next to each other in the same room. During the winter they would go on expeditions in their mink coats, their big felt hats, and their fur-lined shoes, arm in arm, to the ninth floor of Eaton's where they would partake of the buffet of roast beef and petits fours, complete with starchy waitresses, in a setting that looked like a steamship at the beginning of the century, full of art deco, like the *Titanic* before the iceberg. The two old ladies pictured themselves on a cruise, sailing the ocean to see pièces montées and headcheese on the far shore. That was their Apollo 11, a toe on the moon and the feeling they were conquering the universe.

Once the meal was over, they moved slowly along Sherbrooke Street to the Saguenay, the towering building where they had always lived, and whose height confirmed their feeling of being above the crowd. That is, until the wave of foreign newcomers transformed the face of the city and invaded their tower, and the ancient aunts found fertile ground for endless recrimination.

The old ladies were accompanied by an ever-longer list of rules to obey, sit straight, don't put your elbows on the table, handle the silver in the proper fashion, say hello and answer any questions in a restrained voice, wear your hair short or bobbed and be well dressed. Jeanne and Réjeanne knitted out of resentment, one row plain, one row purl, happiness was no requisite. They hadn't known it and after them the deluge, the same fate awaited the younger daughters, my grandmother, my mother, and me at the end of the line.

They were dead by the time the ninth floor of Eaton's was closed, sacrificed to the market economy and replaced by displays of cut-rate bargains. They left the world, first one, then the other, claimed by two different cancers. Their death inspired little sadness, only a cloud of compassion for my grandmother who, as she liked to say, was now a woman without a family. I don't know if my grandmother and her sisters Jeanne and Réjeanne had been wild little girls like that nasty Sophie whose misfortunes they cited to inspire me to cut the heads off goldfish, eat the horses' bread, and torture a doll. There are so many good bad ideas. I wondered if Jeanne and Réjeanne hadn't spent their younger years doing just those things.

One day at school, just before summer vacation, the principal stood on the stage in the gym as all the children watched, and announced that the girl who lived with her aunt and uncle at the end of the field behind our place, near the big pile of gravel that had been left there for no good reason, had disappeared. It wasn't a rumour, it was true. They'd been looking for her for days. People said, "It's not surprising, but such a shame, they didn't even pay attention to their kids!"

My mother, and she was only half-joking, said it was better not to stray too close to that house because a witch lived there. At first I thought of Hansel and Gretel; Doris must have run away. Then the concern started to grow, more and more people came and went from the house, and police cars had been sent from the next village. There were interviews with the aunt and uncle who had custody of the child. Their clothes were dirty, they were dishevelled, they were questioned as they stood on the gravel that led up to their front door, they were threatened with a trip to the police station. The aunt and the uncle were the same size. They looked like twins in their baggy checked shirts, the cloth pulling around the buttonholes because of their big round bellies. They swallowed their words, they kept their hands in their pockets, cigarettes hung from their lips.

They hadn't lived there long. The house was empty before they got there, an old wooden house, one of the oldest in the town, nobody wanted to live there because people said it was haunted. My mother had heard that they didn't have running water and they did their business in an outhouse hidden at the end of the lot, in the field. From our place, we didn't see anything strange, no white plasmas or will-o'-the-wisps. The uncle drove around in an old red pick-up. The aunt never went outside. Sometimes we'd see her bent over her flowerbeds, where nothing ever grew.

A year later, Doris showed up at school. People said she was their niece, her parents were dead, or they'd abandoned her, she grew up in a travelling circus, or in a trailer on Coney Island in a freak show, with criminals and gypsies. I wondered where she got her name.

Doris had two long teeth that protruded from her oversized jawbone, and her eyes were as dark as her hair. She wore blue jeans that made her behind look rounder and her pants fell wide and dirty onto her Adidas that were too big for her. Once, at the end of the year show, she came up to my mother, who was in charge of our hair-dos. She went to her like a lamb, like a little animal that wants to be petted. My mother picked up the brush. Patiently, breathing softly, she started untangling the mass of hair that was stuck to her head, and full of grease and dandruff. Doris sat on the ground, between her legs, with her eyes closed. My mother made two braids, and held them with barrettes, then she put makeup on her. Doris was transfigured.

And then she disappeared. After the principal's announcement, everyone forgot her. We never found out what happened. Her aunt and uncle stayed in the house at the end of the road behind our bungalow. The only time we saw them was when they drove toward Boundary Road in their pick-up.

One Saturday morning, we met Mom at the cash at the new supermarket. She was doing her food shopping, and before we knew it, she had invited herself to our place. She told my mother, "I'll get the stuff out of the car and come and see you!" Then she pushed her buggy toward the exit. As if she wanted to get to the bottom of something, or tell my mother a secret, something important about the village. My mother stood there with her mouth open.

The annual parish celebrations were coming up, and Mom had always organized them. But this year, she was off to a late start. Nothing had been done yet. No one knew why, but the preparations hadn't gotten off the ground. Mom was born here, and all her family was too, parents, grandparents, great-grandparents, the whole family tree. Everyone knew that but no one asked questions. Anyway, nothing good could ever come from this place.

An hour later, Mom was knocking at the door. She came in, sat down at the dining room table with her cup of Sanka without looking at us, then she started in talking. She talked with her head down. It was like she was confessing, but we could hear the warning in what she was saying. She muttered something about this being a village of curses. Her hands shook as she held her cup of coffee. She lowered them and wiped them on her thighs, balled them into fists, then started all over again. A few minutes later, she whispered to my mother that she had something to tell her. My mother sat down in front of her and motioned me to go somewhere else. I left the room. I went into the living room, on the other side, then, quietly, I retraced my steps. I sat down at the base of the wall between the living room and the kitchen with my knees under my chin, and I listened to what Mom was saying.

It happened in the kitchen in the big white house that stood at the edge of the village. The place was abandoned now, the wood was all rotten, the paint peeled away, Daddy was going to demolish it soon and put up something new. I never saw Mom cry except that one time, when she told her grandmother's story, the woman who lived her life in that big white house. Back then, mothers bathed their children in big metal tubs that made the same sound as tin cowbells. The cows were spots against the green of the meadows, they got them at the end of the day and brought them back to the barn in case there was a storm. Élisabeth used the warm afternoons to bathe her kids. She was getting on, thirty-five years of country life and feeling every day of it, thirty-five years of boiled dinners and pot roasts. She never took off her apron, except in the dark at night when she undressed quickly at the foot of the bed, her back to her husband.

That day her husband went out and she wasn't thinking about him. There was a time she thought too much about him, but now it was over. She acted like he wasn't there, she wasn't going to lose a night's sleep over him anymore. She knew he was at the far end of the field, he'd gotten down from the tractor, and next to him, in the tall grass he refused to cut, the earth was drinking up the contents of a bottle that would never be the last. She didn't hear him any more, she didn't recognize the sound of his voice. It had been a while now, his words were undone by drunkenness, the monosyllables of childhood, no one knew what he was trying to say, she let him talk and didn't listen. The kids came into the kitchen after playing with the chickens and the rabbits. They were covered in dust. "Come on! It's time to get washed!" she told them.

The oldest daughter went first, they left her alone in the kitchen so she'd have a little privacy to protect her young breasts and pubic hair, the rest of them pointed their fingers and asked, "Am I going to get that way too?" When she finished, the younger girls climbed into the tub one by one and stood up in it, rocking from side to side, shivering in the summer heat, as their mother poured a pot of water over their heads. To warm up, they would shake like excited puppies, push and shove, splash water on their sisters standing on the floor nearby. When the filth left their skin and was washed into the water, it burst the soap bubbles. Soon, beneath their feet, they felt the sand that had built up in the tub, the sand from the dunes along the river where their girls dug holes all day. Once they came running back to the house, out of breath, proudly showing their mother a bone they found. "It's gotta be a dinosaur bone!" Élisabeth was not impressed by their discovery and replied, "It's the bone of a cow that some very hungry wolf ate, or maybe monsieur Séguin's goat nibbled on it."

When she decided her daughters were clean, with one strong arm she would pull them from the tub and lay them on a towel. Laughter splashed the room. She grabbed her lower back in pain, her eyes were closed, suffering twisted her face. She wiped her forehead. Her youngest was the last, her favourite, probably, the girl who closed off eternity.

Élisabeth grabbed Georgette under the armpits. After the others, she seemed so light. Georgette was her little angel. She had turned three. Her last tooth just came in. Sometimes she thought her daughter was too sweet to find her way in the world and this tribe of savages. She tried to teach her how to count, one two three four when they were all sitting at the table, she pointed at the older girls who had stopped fighting for her attention now that they had other things to talk about.

Georges came back from the fields. She heard the door open behind her. "Papa!" the next to last girl shouted and ran to the screen door to rub her nose against the muddy Wrangler's, the chlorophyll that gives green stains, and the manure spots. A light cloud of whiskey hung around the man. "Here!" said the mother without looking at him. "Change the water." With one arm, Georges pushed aside the little girl who ran to him, picked up the tub, and stumbled toward the sink. Élisabeth left the room. She heard water running. The kids went back to their game with the wet towels. Georgette was calm. She watched her father and waited, her naked skin in the sun that was starting to drift downward in the sky and turn an orange colour. She was a patient child. She never cried, she would put her thumb in her mouth and watch time go by.

In the children's room at the back of the house, Élisabeth was putting away the clothes she'd fixed, the needle moving in and out of the light cotton, then she chose what Georgette would wear. She lived in a house that was full of things. Some days, she would hide a few minutes in the outhouse, at the end of the field. She had gone to school a few years, she could read, a neighbour lady lent her a book that belonged to her father, an old book bound in leather with dog-eared edges. She would hide it in a newspaper and disappear into the yard. She would read a few lines from it before getting on with her day. Afterward, she would catch herself dreaming. She would remember the handsome boy from her girlhood, the one who left too soon because the war called and he died there, she had to stop waiting, take the first guy who asked, the one who looked silly with his cap on.

In the bedroom, suddenly she heard screams. It was like Georgette had climbed back inside her. The screams filled everything. She ran out of the bedroom. When she got there, her youngest was hanging over the edge of the tub. She told herself she hadn't drowned, she was still breathing, then she came right next to her and felt the steam on her face, she saw her skin the colour of poppies and her eyes upturned and white. She grabbed Georgette and pulled her from the water. It was so hot it burned her hands. On the floor, motionless, squatting down, was the father. A neighbour drove them to the nearest hospital. Her youngest died a few days later in silence and suffering, from third-degree burns. The whole village was scandalized. The family turned into an object of curiosity. They couldn't fall any lower. The father left and no one ever saw him again.

Mom sniffed, grabbed a handkerchief, and took off her glasses to dry her eyes. No one has lived in the big white house since. Of the family, she was the only one who didn't leave the village, and sometimes, when she comes out of church, old people remind her of the past. They tell her that Manon-just-Manon reminds them of Georgette, like a bad omen.

The Suburbs

After Doris disappeared and Mom paid her visit, as my mother was peeling potatoes for Saturday lunch, suddenly she broke the silence and said, practically shouting, "We're going to leave this damned place!" It was a formal announcement, an official statement, and there was nothing we could do to make her change her mind. My mother had had it with the stink of manure and boiled chicken gizzards, and that was that. Silence settled over us again. She didn't say where we were going. I felt the tears on my cheeks, I couldn't tell if they were from sadness or relief, then I crossed my fingers and begged God to send us to a city, a real one, New York or Hollywood. I asked her what would become of me. She said, "It's not what you achieve. What matters is leaving the place you came from."

Anjou, Ontario. I never thought we would leave it. I never pictured myself anywhere else. I mourned the memory of my first kiss, I mourned for Manon-just-Manon and spin the bottle, and as the tears ran down my cheeks, my mother raised her eyes to heaven as she was washing the dishes and said, "There's plenty more where that came from." I was pitiful and discouraged. Life was hell, and that was nothing new. After Elvis died, we figured things couldn't get worse, we had scraped the bottom of the barrel like in the beginning of time when Jesus died, and now everything was going crazy again. We had put a man on the moon, Elvis was dead, we were going to move, I didn't know what people meant when they talked about progress.

Then suddenly, for a moment in the noonday sun that poured in through the window above the kitchen sink, my mother stopped scrubbing. She leaned over and whispered to me, like a secret, that the city was full of the future, things I couldn't even imagine. I would need to get used to it. Who knows what I would find there, and who knows how my life would change? She was sure of it, I could hear it in her voice. But deep down, none of that meant anything to me. I had to follow. Parents came and went. We'd come here though we could have gone anywhere, city mice or country, ants or grasshoppers.

I wasn't from the village, I wasn't from anywhere else, but I'd ended up sending down roots among the cornfields and wild strawberries. Sitting on the white swing attached to a blue metal unit that my parents had set up in the backyard, I dreamed of the love of my life and religious devotion, I got dizzy spinning round and round, rolling and unrolling the heavy, rusty chains until I felt sick to my stomach. Maybe one day I would just take off from all that turning in circles, or lose my head, just enough so I wouldn't know where I was.

We had come to the village six years earlier, on Labour Day. We left it six years later, in the middle of summer, for a new start. It was a beautiful hot day. We packed up and left behind the shed where the lawn mower, the shovels, the lawn fertilizer, the grass seed never sown, the place where in winter we set the rabbit hutches so the rabbits wouldn't freeze on the cold nights. We said goodbye to the dirty yellow kitchen linoleum, the white wallpaper in the living room where you could make out dark shadows of the tall trunks of dead trees, and the plywood screwed to the wall in my room so I could stick up and take down the posters of the stars whenever I felt like it. We turned our backs on the church and the parish celebrations, the poker tables, the Ferris wheel, the apple-bobbing where you nearly drowned. I waved goodbye to the car washes in the firehouse garage, and the dance-o-thons in the community hall with amplifiers up to the ceiling.

We left behind the blackened marshmallows, the igloos dug in the snow, the pans of green beans and the paring knife, the mosquito bites, the fat black spiders lying on the bedspread, the leatherette sofa that burned your thighs in summer, the Saturday evening dinners in the mellow light of a Tiffany lamp with every shade of blue, the dips we'd eat in the church basement after first communion or a funeral, the recorder lessons the Gray Sisters gave in their convent, the illustrated Bible in a four-volume set, Jehane Benoît's treasury of recipes, my grandmother's fudge cake and her nut squares, the chicken livers with green peppers, cleaning the blackboards in every classroom in the middle of a snowstorm when there were more absent than present, the dark night of power failures, the red rubber balls with their bumpy lines that we'd play with in the chalk squares in the playground, the fat grey rat we spotted from afar one morning in front of the neighbours' door, the schoolteacher's husband who'd had all his teeth taken out at once and replaced with false ones, and who'd bled like a stuck pig for a week, the circular bungalow that had been built at the edge of the village and where someone finally opened a restaurant for more discriminating diners who ate dishes with thick sauces and crustaceans as if that were the most normal thing in the world. We stole away like thieves in the night. A moving van pulled up and took the furniture and the cardboard boxes, we piled everything else inside the red Cortina and made sure we didn't forget anything so we wouldn't have to return. We left and we never came back, except once or twice because we had nothing better to do than contemplate the past and pat ourselves on the back because we escaped it.

"Get a move on!" said my mother, giving me a gentle shove. "It's time to go!" The sun was shining in a splendid sky, it was hot already like the most torrid summer days, the hell of a peeling nose and sticky skin, we opened the windows as we drove along the 417. I told myself this was the last time I'd see the green sign at the border on the highway. The car went down the road by the corpses of raccoons and skunks, in a landscape of silos. My mother hadn't put Jean-Pierre Ferland's greatest hits in the tape player. Her eyes were elsewhere, she was quiet, she listened to the wind blow. Her skin was shiny with the heat. She was leaning on the elbow rest, her head against her hand. She closed her eyes and opened them, then closed them again with a sigh.

I watched everything go by, the houses, the railroad tracks, the school, the church, the campground, the credit union, the stones, the poplars. Just as we were leaving, we heard BB's mother screaming. The neighbours across the way pointed as they watched our red Cortina go by. Manon-just-Manon turned her back. I didn't know who would live in the bungalow instead of us. Probably a family who didn't have the means to buy a house anywhere else but in this hole. You have to start somewhere.

My parents went from the village to a neighbourhood of row houses, not too close but not too far from the big city, something perfectly average with the British name of Chichester, in the suburbs of our nation's capital.

During the weeks of summer, in my new room and my new bed placed against the new wallpaper with pale, rose-coloured flowerets that my mother had picked out, I associated with the monsters of insomnia. In the next room, my parents' bedroom, I heard the voices of the television. When I sensed that sleep had overtaken them, I went and turned off the set, and the light, took off their glasses, and put them on the bedside table. I went back to my bed and lay down in darkness and stared at the ceiling, waiting for exhaustion to be stronger than everything I could imagine.

I ended up falling asleep in the dead of night, dreaming of what might be waiting for me the next day, the thousand flavours of Baskin-Robbins in a sugar cone and the fear of losing my way. It was a jungle out there in front of McDonald's, at the corner of Ogilvy and Montreal Road.

The neighbourhood with its attached houses was a miniature world like Madurodam, the tiny model of Holland in Scheveningen. Alice in Wonderland after she read *Drink Me*. It was a world where you felt protected, little girls absorbed by their sculptures in the sandbox, carefree, their lifted dresses showing their underpants, blue, pink, and white. They told each other about their day, hallucinating about a land where fairies flitted like butterflies, breathing in the sun, bringing children sweet visions of sleep. Their voices rose like little birds, the sound of crystal against the façades.

In my room, in the evening, I would listen to their voices for hours, in summer the sun sets late, I wondered when silence would finally come over them like a shower that would send them inside, their parents calling, "Quick, you'll get soaked." When their voices disappeared, my fear would take over, and I would wait for a sudden noise. People said they weren't worried in this neighbourhood of attached houses, nothing ever happened here, it was an ideal place to live, no problem.

It was a suburb within a suburb, between the rock of the village and the hard place of the city, a space of transition. We knew everything about the neighbours. The vertical blinds left open in the picture windows displayed the décor, the choice of colours, materials, and objects. Nothing escaped the eye. All the interiors were the same, despite the different models scattered through the body of the housing complex. On all sides the walls were so thin that the neighbours' lives were close to ours, the steps on the staircase, the laughter, the sounds in the night. Behind the houses were little yards separated by a shared fence, and at the back of the yard, the garages where the cars slept at night until morning freed them, "Hello, watch

out for the sun, watch out for the rain, have a nice day!"
On the weekend came the song of the hoses that cleansed
the car bodies of the week's dust. At times, squealing tires
because a bike hadn't been put away or a child had run
into the street to catch up to a ball. The speed limit was
clearly indicated, speed bumps everywhere, no dozing off
at the wheel, vigilance demanded, alcohol blood levels
strictly monitored.

Here, all fires were banked. We lived in slow motion,
in an atmosphere of mutual respect and support, good re-
lations and harmony. In the evening, coming back from
work on public transit that practically dropped us on our
front step, at the corner of two main arteries, we would
pay our neighbours a visit for cocktails, dips and olives,
whatever was on hand. During vacation, Thanksgiving,
Christmas, in the summer, we organized potlatches like
the Indians, and sometimes, further into the city, we went
on secretive treasure hunts. In the summer, the kids gathered at the public pool. Their parents had signed them
up for swimming classes so they would learn to survive
in water so cold it made them shiver. The smaller ones
cried when they were left in the arms of the lifeguards,
but once the first shock had passed, they splashed merrily
in complete safety as their babysitters closed their eyes behind their sunglasses, escaping in their bathing suits into
the flamboyant world of superstars. The concrete tiles ran
with water. The floor in the shower room was sticky. The
metal door squealed, and the sound set our teeth on edge.
At noon, we left the compound that had gotten too hot,

and returned two hours later, in the cool of the afternoon. Then, after that, a little T-shirt and a towel around our shoulders to ease the goose bumps raised by the evening breezes, except when the dog-day heat lingered.

We stayed as long as we could, putting off the time when we'd have to go home, the family dinner and the household chores to teach children what life was really like. "You'll understand when you get older." We didn't see the sun go down. The horizon was just a concept behind the row houses, the hill that ran down to the wealthier suburb with its large houses, yellow, white, and blue, that looked like papier mâché.

We had just moved when the year 1984 arrived like a blockbuster or the Last Judgement. Tino Rossi was dead, Nathalie Simard stopped eating Laura Secord pudding, Céline Dion sang *Une colombe* for the Pope, copies of *Christiane F* were handed out like a vaccination against bad ideas. Life was like a pause between wars with no hope that the men might return, without roses stuck in the mouths of cannons. The bodies piled up, memories were left to rot to fertilize plastic flowers. Mothers considered pain a capricious luxury. They said, "Out of the mouth of teenagers does not come the truth. No sense rushing, everything comes to those who wait. Young hearts heal faster." They promised to be nonchalant, but the fear remained, the mothers closing their eyes in the face of danger. And we waited, caught in time that was sticky like the eye of a soft watch, in front of the TV where we watched wicker cradles floating down the rivers of Asia, frail bodies sold to the women who kept brothels and to tourists who knew how to find the right spots without Lonely Planet. People said there were as many Ophelias in the Hudson River as empty bottles and dirty Kleenexes.

The antechamber of the city would be the antechamber of adult life, adolescence was a circle of hell and so were the suburbs. There was a common logic between the row houses and the polyester uniforms of the private school whose doors I would soon march through. To prepare for September, so I wouldn't be afraid when I crossed the city on the bus, my mother made a dry run with me. I wasn't used to public transit. The only time I had taken it was with an old lady who looked after me and took me under her wing during the summer, whose own children lived far from the village. They'd left it as soon as possible and made their lives in the city.

The private school was a former convent. The teachers were half-defrocked priests who swore by the Lord, though they could not give up their sins. They prowled the hallways, moving along the walls through the student body, as if we had penetrated a sacred place.

I was still a kid when I started private school. I didn't add up to much next to the girls who had just turned teenagers, but who could pass for eighteen, like Chantal Brunet whose shapely beauty everyone admired. She had long hair, big eyes, incisors that overlapped a little in the middle, her face was covered with a thick layer of foundation that described a dark circle along her jawbone and under her chin. Her eyelashes, draped in mascara, looked like long, hairy spider legs. She applied blue powder to her eyelids and drew along the inside with a black pencil. In the corner of her eye, the result looked like a mass of greyish secretions. Chantal Brunet had breasts and a handbag. She curled her hair and could walk on high heels without falling.

I had Christine Blondin in my class too. We were

practically neighbours, and we took the same bus in the morning. She was much taller than I was and very pretty too, with dark eyes and hair and a dark complexion. She smiled all the time, a smile that made you think her childhood was behind her already. One of the drawers of my memory has her mixed up with Céline Dion, like two socks the same colour, but not the same pattern. Christine was prettier.

I would go to her house after school. She lived on the other side, at the bottom of the hill, on the road to the shopping centre, in a luxury split-level. We lived in a narrow row house inside a housing complex divided into little squares. It was a small society, a Lego town, a Playmobil village. Christine lived in the real world, with a house standing on a real street, beneath trees that had had time to mature. I can't picture her room. I never saw her father, who was a senior civil servant and travelled all the time, but I remember the kitchen and her little brother who drove his tricycle over the linoleum, in concentric circles around his mother. He was too blond to be true, an angel from heaven.

Christine was sweet, happy, and too nice. Sometimes her face would get a sad look, but it never lasted. She was a little slow, as if a thread held her back in the naivety of childhood and kept her from understanding the unseen side of things, irony, metaphors, double meanings, and that in this world there were bad people too. When she looked after kids, babysitting for parents who went out for the evening, she played with the children without self-consciousness or boredom, she participated completely in the games of hide-and-seek and fancy dress, building a tent with lengths of fabric draped over the furniture.

Christine was a bridge between the stages of life. At first you would say she was eighteen, then her laughter would betray her, she laughed like a little bird, a child. Her brown eyes shone and when a shadow fell over them, it was because of some disappointment, like kids who sulk when they've been refused candy. Christine was someone whose purity people wanted to preserve, a sort of village simpleton who wasn't quite that simple and who didn't wander aimlessly through the streets. She would believe anything about film stars and extraterrestrials. We had to read *The Chrysalis* in English class, and she believed every word. She listened, attentive, trusting, never questioning the interpretations she was given. She had the goodness of people who don't understand and who don't think that the person talking to them could turn out to be bad.

Christine attracted boys. She had a woman's body, and they all managed to find a way to touch it, even if it was only once, a single time, because afterwards you had to be ready to protect her, and not be ashamed that she was a little slow. I was like the others: little by little, I drifted away from her.

Years later, my mother told me that Christine Blondin had started going out with the Governor General's son, the one who went on to work with the handicapped. Sometime after that, when I stopped at the house during summer vacation, which always felt like a return to childhood, my mother told me Christine's things had been found scattered around a street corner near the house, by the shelter where for years I would get off the bus and walk home trembling because it was midnight. Christine had disappeared. It didn't happen in New York, it happened here, in this neighbourhood where nothing ever happened, where you had to invent everything so you wouldn't die of boredom because you'd forgotten to breathe.

She was never found. She had cancelled her afternoon shift at work, and the next morning her parents noticed she hadn't come back that night and hadn't taken her purse. People said that one of her teachers saw her running through the intersection. That was the day she disappeared, at the end of the afternoon.

Meanwhile, on the world's surface, in the heart of its tiny navel, the Calgary Olympics were going on. Everyone was talking about them and the tainted blood scandal, AIDS and transfusions, the signature from another time. Then the local paper went on strike, and on TV they didn't talk about such

82

things. It's like she'd disappeared twice, once on the street, a second time everywhere else. Years later, a bag of human bones was found at the bottom of the river. The detectives tried to find out which of the three women it was, all tall, with brown hair and dark complexions, all having disappeared one after the other over a period of a few weeks, near the row houses.

I imagine the parents growing older, wrinkles and white hair, life going on despite them because when you've given life it's hard to see it flicker out. They wouldn't leave their suburban house, who knows if their daughter might come back some day, as if that could ever happen, and she would knock on their door, she'd have forgotten her key, a tentative knock so as not to disturb them, they might be sleeping. I picture time, heavy and thick, the time that goes by uncounted except for what it writes on their bodies, and they can't do anything about it, the skein of delicate lines around their eyes and lips, the habit of smiling still written on their faces, despite it all.

These days, on the Internet you can see an archive picture of her posted by a network that will not let the Jane Does fall into the black hole of forgetting. The parents must feel the pain on Christmas Day, and the face of the little brother who became a famous actor here, a blond colossus with an innocent look, though hot to trot, a Houdini of stage and screen. No way to know whether he is waiting for her too, if he thinks of her constantly or tries to forget a little until it returns to haunt him like a poorly buried ghost. Once, as he searches for some obscure source to feed the pain of one of his characters, perhaps he'll think of her, and she will come and drape a length of velvet over his eyes, very soft, very black.

At the end of the line of houses perpendicular to ours, on the western side of the sandbox, stood Nathalie's house. She went to the private high school too, with her little beige skirt with a pleat in the middle and an old man's brown jacket. When she got back home in the evening, she pulled on her skin-tight jeans and her flowered shirt and tied a length of black leather around her neck. Nathalie was a real rocker girl. She lived with her brother, her mother, and her mother's girlfriend – the one who'd shown up in their life after the father disappeared. They said he died in the war, but no one could say which one or whether it was really true. She lived in a house full of dried flowers, woven things, ceramics, and hanging gardens.

One time I left my house and slammed the door, it was Saturday afternoon, my parents were washing the new puppy they'd gone to get at the breeder's during the week. I ran away for an hour or two, it was pathetic, really, I hid out at Nathalie's. I rang and she opened the door, she was alone. Her mother and her stepmother had gone out with her noisy little brother. Nathalie was more than happy to see me. We took our places in the living room like ladies sitting down to tea, she gave me something to eat and drink. The house smelled like freshly baked cookies, it was like the smell in the convent when I went there for piano lessons, but I wasn't hungry, my stomach was in knots. I was angry, and carrying on, I stamped my foot, to hell with this suburb, it was no better than the village, I'd never go back home….

Nathalie listened to me and didn't say anything. She came from a big city, a real one, and she didn't care. I didn't know what she had left behind, but she gave me the feeling she'd never been lonely. She wasn't afraid of anything, a mysterious force stood by her and revealed something more than what I knew, it didn't come from men, or women, or dogs. She curled up deep in the sofa as I talked, her arms around her knees, and I was next to her. The sun lit up the house, the exposure was better than in our place, the embroidered pillows that accented the couch were warm. I picked up one of them and held it against my breast like a shield. There was nothing for me in the heart of these row houses, nothing but the swimming pool up on the little hill as a point to look to.

When I stood in front of our door and didn't know where to go, when I didn't know what to do with my day, my mother lost patience and told me to stop. She said I was old enough to know what I wanted. I bit my fingers, I cracked my knuckles, I waited for a sign from heaven, something that would clearly show me what direction to go in. Near the sandbox, in the middle of the block of row houses, there was no horizon. I lifted my eyes in search of it, but in vain. Above the red brick façades and the well-drawn roads, I knew there was an intersection, the shopping centre, the roads that led to another suburb, the highway, and downtown Ottawa. But I saw nothing. I didn't know if life began or ended with the bus shelter and the traffic lights. It was like a cauldron, a Presto with its cover tightly screwed on. Even God didn't have the power to open it. The village was suffering, the suburb, absence, the absence of place. Banishment.

Nathalie told me how her mother and her stepmother organized séances with their girlfriends, the dead would come and pay them a visit, all kinds of dead people within the new walls of the row houses. I wondered about the ground the suburb had been built on. I wondered who would come and speak to them that way. I pictured a scene from a film, a storm raging and the electricity going off, the velvety darkness, the lit candles. I saw women holding hands, their eyes closed, open to the invisible beings who moved through them, their voices replaced by someone else's who had something important to tell them. I wondered what use that was, what would remain of all that in the future? Once Nathalie joined in. She met someone, a girl her age who had lived in the neighbourhood and floated among us without our seeing her. Nathalie said she had often felt a presence close by, a kind of warmth. A face would appear to her at night on her bedroom wall, and she didn't know if it was a dream, a girl with blond curls wearing a lace collar like in my favourite book when I was a child, where the heroine found theatre sets and costumes in her grandparents' attic. Nathalie said she looked like a porcelain doll, a pale Pierrot with velvet clothing and ribbons for decoration.

We never found out who the phantom girl was. Maybe

Nathalie dreamed her up after what her mother told her some time earlier about the child she had lost, the girl who would have been her eldest and who left her belly after twenty weeks without anyone ever knowing she'd left where she had been, why she had made that choice. That was the way Nathalie's mother talked about the child, and Nathalie felt less lonely, the wing of an angel lay across her shoulders and protected her.

Nathalie's house seemed different to me after she told me her story. It became a place of both disquiet and repose. I wanted to have access to the little girl who had disappeared too, but I wasn't going to think about it too much, these things couldn't be forced. It was like having the vocation for religion. You could pray all you wanted, it came from somewhere hidden and all you could do is just have faith.

When I told her about Nathalie, my mother looked away, and she frowned. I said I wanted books on the subject, about the dead and telepathy, those things interested me a lot. She dismissed me lightly, and said it was just an adolescent passion, and it would pass. Nathalie's stories were all that remained of mystery in the disciplined world of row houses. That, and the circumstances surrounding Marilyn Monroe's death. Sitting in front of the legendary photo with the white dress that I'd pinned to my bedroom wall, I read a cheap paperback about a detective who claimed to have the proof that it was murder.

Another weekend, in the middle of the morning, the phone rang and it was Nathalie. My mother handed me the receiver, I was watching TV, and I heard my friend's trembling voice saying, "I had a vision, could you go see and make sure the house isn't on fire?" I said, "Yes, I promise," then I hung up. My mother was standing next to me, and I told her. I didn't know whether I should believe Nathalie, even though I'd given her my word. I blushed when I was talking to her, I didn't really believe her, and my mother ended up saving me. She didn't hesitate a second. The house was right next door, it wouldn't cost anything, we'd go check. I was relieved and looked at her with admiration, like the time I came home after Marcel the neighbour boy pulled down his pants in front of me and she didn't bat an eyelash when I told her. "It happens all the time, every kid does that." I felt like I'd gotten away with something.

My mother would have the right perspective. She wasn't absent, but she did have distance. Often ironic, often critical, most of the time benevolent, she watched me build who I was at some remove, sticking together the mismatched pieces and trying to see what image they would provide. She didn't try to replace the lost piece of the puzzle, she let me live with loss. We didn't talk about it, it had minimal existence. She'd had love with him and motherhood with me, between him and me there was a story to write, but she wouldn't be the one to write it. It was all about faith, here too. A missing father existed on the other side of the ocean, the way you had to believe in Christ without thrusting your hand into his side like Thomas. The relation was between him and me. My mother didn't get in the way.

My theatre teacher helped me understand that. I'd started cleaning her house to make a little money. She explained that my mother hadn't taken anything away from me. It was the opposite: she'd stepped aside to leave me the freedom to choose what I wanted for the future, a missing father or a found one. The teacher was a middle-age woman who would soon retire from the private school. She had sad eyes and lived alone in a row house in another housing complex at the bottom of the hill, behind the pool. I took dramatic arts classes with her. She liked me and asked if I wanted to be her cleaning lady.

The walls of her house were white. She had very little furniture. Everything was very neat. On her bedroom walls were two pencil drawings of Indian chiefs. Once when I was running the feather duster over her night tables, she told me they were her ancestors. I listened quietly as she told the story: the faces had appeared to a medium, which is how she recovered her origins. Her parents, who had adopted her from a Montreal orphanage after the Second World War, had no idea where she came from. She had looked all her life, searched her memory for pebbles that might have been forgotten, until one day a girlfriend suggested a séance. She let herself go, and had been transported by the eyes of those who had been vehicles for others and now translated their story.

I cleaned her house after school, every Friday. She gave me a key. One evening, it was winter, someone rang at the door. I went to see and there she was, covered in blood. She had fallen on the icy steps and hit her head. Her dyed blond hair was stained, her fingers, her gloves, the front of her coat, and she was delirious. I called an ambulance and with the cleaning half done, I rode to the hospital with her. We waited hours in Emergency, she on a stretcher, me on a straight-backed chair. When she recovered her wits, she told me to leave. It was time to go home, it was dark already.

I never saw her again after that. It was like I had witnessed some forbidden event. What happened had everything and nothing to do with me. One day she had told me that when children split open their head or their face when they fall, they are freed of something. I figured that something had left her too, some great despair or a demon. I didn't know what I was going to retain of all that, but I never returned to her house.

The City

The next year, even if it was too soon, I took the bus to downtown Ottawa and the apartment I would be sharing with a girl who was ten years older than me, with long, wavy hair, antiques in her room, a married lover, and a venereal disease. She agreed to rent me her spare bedroom as a transition between my parents' house and real freedom. I put a single bed, my parents' old kitchen table, some books stuck in an old cupboard, and all my innocence into that room. It was a half-basement in a luxury building, my window looked onto the parking lot, and I woke up in the middle of the night with the carbon monoxide.

My mother watched me go with a grim look, not trying to hold me back, but letting me know that returning wouldn't be simple for me, life would never be as it was before. I was leaving for life in the city, to study by day and work at night, coming home late along Somerset Street as if danger didn't exist. Sometimes, for several days, my roommate wouldn't come home, and I started to get worried. I made up all kinds of stories, maybe she'd been kidnapped, or met the love of her life, or become a prostitute. When she reappeared, her face drawn and tired, I asked her to please tell me her plans next time. She shrugged her shoulders, she didn't know why I cared about her, and she went to wash off her adventures in the shower.

I envied her freedom, her elegance, and even her depressed evenings spent languorously in front of the TV screen, watching everything and nothing. On those nights I was relegated to my room, and my boring life spent in the hot light of my desk lamp. I felt like I was living with a movie star. Sometimes, when she was away, I would venture into her bedroom, my heart beating fast. I opened the little drawers of her circular armoire and gazed lovingly at her pearls, golden chains, and medallions that fell in waves like her long hair when she untied her chignon. Her underthings lay on the floor, stockings and black tights on the enormous bed covered with a pure white duvet with an embroidered hem like in the old days. She owned tons of clothes, all mismatched, which she put together with astonishing results. At Christmas, I gave her a pretty white silk scarf with black polka dots that I had bought for my mother before changing my mind, once I realized I had chosen wrong. Delighted, she lifted the heavy mass of her hair and draped the scarf around her neck, and I thought she was beautiful despite the dark circles under her eyes and the exhaustion that had begun preying on her body. She was beautiful the way my mother had been one particularly warm Easter day, in her long white rayon dress dotted with bright flowers that clung to her body perfectly.

The years passed and I heard that she had had a son who was already inside her when I gave her the scarf, the married man had deposited the child in her belly without realizing, and she was waiting for the right time to tell him. Later, I understood that she had raised him on her own, the father there once a week, once a month, then once a year.

That was our only Christmas together. The next spring, I left her apartment and moved in with a girlfriend who brought home a Canadian reservist whose black boots punished the floor at all hours of the night. Since the territory was occupied, I decided to leave the apartment, then the city, and finally deserted the country. I moved further from the village in ever-larger concentric circles. I ended up in a completely white apartment in Ann Arbor, Michigan, then in a two-room unaffordable flat in the depths of Southampton, England. I landed in Montreal years later. When it came time to decide in what neighbourhood I would set down my suitcases, I made one last detour. I flew off to the big city I'd seen on TV.

I had watched loads of films, dramas of disappearance and murder, waiting rooms with walls dark with mould, squalling emergency rooms packed to the ceiling, metallic morgues, the grey faces of young policemen either corrupt or callous, impassive behind a rusty grill at the station door, telling mothers, as they looked away, "We'll call you as soon as there's anything new in the case." I was saturated with such images.

It was after September 11th. Ghosts were running every which way, potent, enraged, deafening. I left for a few days, figuring nothing much would happen, nothing bad produced by Fox News or Universal, no premonitions, no conspiracies. I held my breath as the plane took off, I had listened to the story of the taxi driver's divorce, his daughters at private school with their scholarships, him disporting himself with certain lady customers with special tastes. I watched New York appear at the end of the bridge like a gigantic wedding cake.

The evening I got there, a pack of cops had taken up position at the edge of the park by Columbus Circle, standing with one hand on their hips, their legs slightly open, in combat attitude. *We're trying to prevent something from happening.* The next morning at dawn, a guy on a bike in a ski mask set off a bomb in Times Square, in front of a US Army recruitment centre. It wasn't the first time that had happened. There had been other attacks, but this time they took him seriously. Sent out into the streets, journalists took the collective pulse of the population, they questioned the man in the street. "Have we lost our innocence forever?" they asked.

On the evening news, proud and amazed, the anchorman remarked on New Yorkers' imperturbable coolheadedness. For those who had experienced the worst, life went on despite everything, *it's a wonderful world, it's a beautiful day in the USA.* On the TV, I watched young mothers calmly pushing their baby strollers down the numbered streets, schoolgirls in uniform hanging out in Chelsea and Washington Square. Groups of girls paraded by the kiosk in the heart of Central Park, old women were quietly knitting on a bench, their shoulders touching, each one bent over her work. A stitch in time saves nine, life goes on, life in its ordinariness.

A young woman stopped at a newsstand, and the man gave her a quick greeting. He knew her, she came by every morning and lingered a few minutes to talk as if she were actually speaking to him. She had been engaging in verbal delirium all her life with, as a background, the orchestra of sirens and horns, shouting out the paranoia that people share but cannot express, even in the lowest of voices. Then the woman moved on, walking quickly down the avenue to her next stop. The newsman lifted his head and organized his papers, he watched her stride into the distance and he sighed. He knew a woman in his country, in Pakistan. All day long, day after day, she walked the same length of sidewalk, between two blocks of houses, as if she were going somewhere. She walked quickly and determinedly to the intersection, then turned around like swimmers at the end of the pool, and continued on her way again. People said that when she was young, she had lost a child. "She was a wealthy woman," said the newsman, "she wasn't like us." Her daughter was never seen again and she never stopped walking. The people in the neighbourhood offered her food and drink, even clothes and new shoes to protect her twisted, bloody feet. They left her things along the wall in front of which they knew she would pass. At night, for an hour or two, when everyone was sleeping, she would stop, but went back to walking as soon as the sun came up.

Tourists complain about New Yorkers. They say they are rude and rough, arrogant and intolerant. Meanwhile, New Yorkers go on leading their lives and ignore the tourists as best they can, and don't bother steering around them when they stop in the middle of a crowd, on the sidewalk to read their maps, gazing skyward and squinting against the sun, taking a photo that everyone has seen ten thousand times. Tourists are sand in the well-oiled machine of the city.

I moved to the rhythm of the city. I went from the Upper West Side down to Battery Park via Ground Zero. The crowds were like a tidal wave, unfurling power, and I let them carry me along. All around, the clicking of high heels, the swinging of leather briefcases at the end of arms, fragments of conversation caught out of the air, the cries of hot dog and newspaper vendors. Walking fast, businessmen wearing Hugo Boss talked at top speed to a partner hidden in an earphone deep in their ears. People moved in and out of restaurants with a slice of pizza, a bagel, a pastrami sandwich, eating as they walked. Some-times they stopped in front of a store window, paused to light a cigarette, sheltered from the wind, then got back in step again. You had to know where you were going, and if you didn't, you had to get out of the crowd to find your bearings. The crowd runs the show.

I followed the sidewalks of New York like a series of blind alleys. When I got to the end of Broadway, I started back the opposite way. This time, I wandered through the small side streets, a labyrinth I discovered one step at a time, knowing I would find my way even if I didn't know where I was going. The streets unrolled before my feet. I moved quickly, almost running, like on a moving stair-way. My own movements were my guide, pushing and pulling me like a bird riding the air currents having given up any direction. The streets were pathways filled with clues for a quest with no object. I moved along them at breakneck speed, seeing practically nothing, feeling the vibrations of other bodies, the music people made, catch-ing hold of life the way you hear the notes of a score. There was no meaning to look for, just movement to fol-low, no race against an imaginary clock.

I moved through the streets of New York with the sun as my only guide. I lost then recovered it, always heading north. A few hours later, on the street in front of me, I recognized the newspaper stand. It was late, the vendor had closed for the day, and I went back to the hotel. The TV news had nothing new to say. The day had been av-erage, nothing serious to report. The criminals were the same as the day before. On the news, they went on counting the soldiers who were dying in a senseless war overseas that raged in the cities, on the roads, in the empty lots. But closer to us, current events had taken the day off.

The next morning, I went back to Montreal.

On the way to JFK Airport, the taxi driver told me about a different army. There was an event much appreciated by tourists, the Mermaid Parade and Ball at Coney Island. It took place once a year with, among others in attendance, Creamy Stevens, Little Brooklyn, Bambi, the Mermaid, Bunny Love, Sizzle Dizzle, and My Name Is Jamie. The Little Mermaid is about a girl who sacrifices her voice for the love of a prince who doesn't recognize her as the one who saved his life during a shipwreck. "Stab him in the heart with this knife!" the five sisters beg of the girl who has sacrificed herself, and you can return to our realm. Unable to do the slightest damage, the Little Mermaid throws the knife into the sea and becomes a daughter of the air.

In the plane, in the thick sky above New York, I looked for the daughters of the air. Maybe they were flying above the city, or floating among the clouds near the Statue of Liberty, like paratroopers for whom the war will never end. Once we reached cruising speed, I watched the flight attendant moving up the aisle. She had performed the demonstration of what to do in case of an emergency and stowed her kit in the baggage compartment at the front of the aircraft. I wondered if, since September 11th, everything had become as complicated as they said, or if nothing would ever be complicated enough. The flight attendant was tall, blond, pretty, and not completely there. Absent-mindedly, she prepared the beverage cart. She was young, but she had already blocked the cart with her foot a thousand times when crossing through a zone of turbulence. She knew how to manoeuvre the vehicle by using her weight, setting cups full of liquid garnished with a plastic stick on the tray tables without spilling a drop. She had deep violet circles under her eyes from the long shifts, and the demanding passengers like the man who called her three times in a half hour for water, coffee, and salted peanuts, and she always answered with a smile, and never an exasperated look.

The story tells us that if they want to be immortal, the daughters of the air must do good deeds for three hundred years. The time can be reduced if, when they enter the houses of men who have children, they come upon a wise child. But if the child is cruel and wicked, every tear he causes to be shed adds a day to their ordeal. That reminded me of the stories told in the village church on Sunday mornings, the same role played by different characters, or in the books of the *Bibliothèque rose* for dutiful young ladies. I liked to imagine the daughters of the air as soldiers for justice, amazons, and like angels too, like sisters, the sisters of mercy, blood sisters, sisters for life, the sisters of providence, of liberty, the sisters of New York City.

In Russia, they say that in every little girl lives a woman, like a doll that has been assembled backwards, with the biggest in the middle. All those girls who had disappeared lived on inside me, and I brought them to light like rabbits jumping out of a magician's hat. I carried them inside the way that widows, the betrothed, sisters, and girlfriends wear the dog tags of a soldier missing in action.

The evening before we left the cursed village, my mother found me bent over a set of small, scattered pieces on the table in my bedroom. Some of them had fallen to the floor, and were lost in the carpet. My fingertips were covered with glue, I didn't know which piece I should stick to create the model of the Lotus Esprit, the car James Bond drove in *The Spy Who Loved Me*. My mother sat on my bed and watched me work for a while. Then she got up, and without a word, kissed me on the head and went back to the kitchen with a sigh, there was so much left to do, emptying the cupboards, packing the boxes, taking out the garbage, not to mention the back she had to turn on the past.

I stayed in the silence of my room. I went on delicately gluing the pieces together. I felt calm and patient. I had discovered the proper order. I saw the light at the end of the tunnel, the last piece and where to place it. It was the hero's car. It could run at top speed along country roads and wide paved avenues, across sand dunes and mountain slopes. It was submersible, and from the bottom of the sea, it could fire rockets.

The day we left, I took my spot on the back seat of the red Cortina. The car went down Boundary Road to the turn-off at the highway. More and more space slipped between us and that pitiful village. As we drove away, I didn't look back once.

MIX
Paper from
responsible sources
FSC® C100212
www.fsc.org

Printed by Imprimerie Gauvin
Gatineau, Québec